A sudden movement in the churned-up mud at the edge of the water hole caught Jake's eye. 'It's an elephant!' he gasped. 'A calf, I think. It's stuck.'

Jake scrambled out of the helicopter. He leaped to the ground, ducked beneath the still whirling blades and charged past Rick towards the stricken calf.

'Hey! What do you think you're doing?' Rick yelled.

'There's a calf stuck in the mud,' Jake shouted back.

'Wait!' Rick ordered.

But Jake kept going. The thick brown mud seemed to want to suck him down into its swampy depths. He looked back to see if Rick was coming, but instead of his stepdad, a huge grey mass filled his view. An elephant was charging straight for him!

Also in the Safari Summer *series*

Pride
Hunted

Other series by Lucy Daniels,
published by Hodder Children's Books

Animal Ark

Animal Ark Pets

Little Animal Ark

Animal Ark Hauntings

Dolphin Diaries

LUCY DANIELS

SAFARI SUMER TUSK

Illustrated by
Pete Smith

*Hodder
Children's
Books*

a division of Hodder Headline Limited

For Richard, Karen, Henry and George Billson,
with lots of love

Special thanks to Andrea Abbott

Thanks also to everyone at the Born Free Foundation
(www.bornfree.org.uk) for reviewing the
wildlife information in this book

Text copyright © 2003 Working Partners Limited
Created by Working Partners Limited, London W6 0QT
Illustrations copyright © 2003 Pete Smith

First published in Great Britain in 2003
by Hodder Children's Books

For more information about Lucy Daniels,
please visit www.animalark.co.uk

10 9 8 7 6 5 4 3 2 1

A Catalogue record for this book is available from
the British Library

ISBN 0 340 85124 4

Typeset in Palatino by Avon DataSet Ltd,
Bidford-on-Avon, Warwickshire

Printed and bound in Great Britain by Clays Ltd, St Ives plc

The paper and board used in this paperback by
Hodder Children's Books are natural recyclable products
made from wood grown in sustainable forests.
The manufacturing processes conform to the environmental
regulations of the country of origin.

Hodder Children's Books
a division of Hodder Headline Limited
338 Euston Road
London NW1 3BH

ONE

Jake Berman swung his racquet at the tennis ball spinning towards him. *Thwack!* The ball soared away, high above the head of his best friend, Shani Rafiki. She stared up at it, her eyes narrowed against the dazzling sun and her racquet dangling helplessly in one hand.

'I'll get it,' Jake offered. He dropped his racquet and raced across the lawn.

'I think it's gone over the fence,' Shani called after him.

'No, it hasn't,' Jake shouted back, pushing his way through the thick bushes that grew next to the three metre high fence. He'd spotted the bright green ball, just out of his reach. 'It's caught in the barbed wire at the top.' He glanced over his shoulder, then started to haul himself up the strong wire mesh. He knew he'd probably be in trouble if his mum,

Hannah, or stepdad, Rick, saw him. After all, there was a very good reason for keeping out the vast African wilderness that lay beyond.

This wilderness was Musabi – a game reserve in Tanzania where Rick was the chief warden. Musabi teemed with wild animals, including the famous African 'big five' – lions, leopards, rhinos, elephants and buffalo.

But Jake didn't think he was putting himself in any real danger right now. His focus was on getting back the tennis ball. He'd already hit two others over the fence that morning, and it wasn't as if he could just cycle up to the local store to buy some more.

Halfway up the fence, Jake was reaching for the ball when something caught his eye – a slight movement among the Mopane trees at the other side of the fence. His first thought was that it was probably a monkey, but as he watched, a branch was pushed aside and a bulky grey shape emerged silently into a clearing just metres away.

'Yikes! Elephant,' Jake gulped as the huge animal lumbered towards him, setting down one massive foot after the other. For a moment, he panicked, not sure what to do. He'd only been living in Africa for a few months, but that had been long enough to teach him that elephants weren't always as gentle as they looked. They could be really dangerous in the wrong mood. Should he let go of the wire and jump down, or keep absolutely still? Rick was always telling him not to move if a wild animal confronted him. Jake glanced down quickly. *Best to jump*, he decided, but he hesitated when he saw that the elephant was now almost at the fence.

Suddenly Jake noticed the elephant's left tusk, which jutted out awkwardly, almost at a right angle. He let out a sigh of relief. 'Oh, it's you, Goliath! You nearly gave me a heart attack.'

Goliath was an orphaned bull elephant that had been raised by keepers at the Rungwa Wildlife Sanctuary. He had been found wandering alone on the savannah when he was only a few months old. Two years ago, at the age of ten, he had come to Musabi, so that he could lead a more natural, independent life in the bush. But his early years had left him very confident around humans, and he often appeared at the Bermans' fence.

Sometimes, Goliath would come crashing through the bushes so noisily that Jake knew that he was around long before he saw him. But at other times, like today, Goliath would appear without making a sound, always taking Jake completely by surprise. There was something very eerie about suddenly finding yourself looking up at the biggest land mammal in the world.

Goliath seemed puzzled to find Jake clinging to the fence. He ambled closer until he was no more than an arm's length away, then stopped and fixed his intelligent dark gaze on Jake.

'Awesome!' Jake exclaimed. Being able to meet the huge animal eye-to-eye was definitely worth the discomfort of the wire digging into the palms of his hands!

Elephant and human locked eyes for a few seconds before Goliath made a deep throaty rumble and, reaching over the fence with his muscular wrinkled trunk, snuffled curiously at Jake's hair.

'OK. That's enough of that,' Jake grinned. Ducking first to one side then to the other to escape the inquisitive trunk, he started to climb back down the fence, the tennis ball forgotten. He'd have liked to stay with Goliath a bit longer, but Rick had warned him not to get too close to the bull. The whole idea of releasing the elephant at Musabi was for Goliath to be less dependent on humans. Also, even though he seemed friendly, he was still a wild animal. And wild animals could be very unpredictable and dangerous, no matter how calm and tame they appeared.

As if to prove this, Goliath suddenly hooked the tip of his trunk around a strand of wire and started to shake the fence violently. Caught by surprise, Jake lost his grip and fell to the ground, landing painfully in a prickly bush. The tennis ball was shaken loose too, and bounced against Jake's forehead.

'Thanks!' Jake muttered, disentangling himself from the bush just as Shani appeared.

'What happened—?' she began, but then she saw Goliath and quietly backed away. 'Oops,' she whispered to Jake. 'I didn't realize he was here. He looks a bit fed up.'

'He's probably on the scrounge again,' Jake said, brushing down his shorts and walking over to join Shani. Goliath famously loved bananas. He'd developed a taste for them when he was growing up at Rungwa. 'But you know that Rick says we're not to encourage him. He's got to start learning to stand on his own two . . . I mean, four feet,' Jake added.

Goliath unhooked his trunk from the wire and started swishing it back and forth along the ground on the other side of the fence, like a big vacuum pipe.

'He's sulking,' Shani chuckled. 'Just like a small kid!'

'It's no good sulking, Goliath,' Jake told him. 'You're supposed to be growing up now.' More sombrely, he added, 'And it's about time you started hanging about with other elephants instead of us all the time.'

Shani wrinkled her nose. 'You'd think he'd have found a friend by now.'

'Rick reckons he will eventually,' Jake said. 'But he's certainly taking his time about it. Sometimes I think he goes out of his way to avoid other elephants.'

There were several herds of elephants in Musabi. Rick had expected Goliath to join one of the herds, or to team up with some other young bulls to form a bachelor herd. But so far, Goliath had shown no interest in any of them.

'You'd think he'd be bored with his own company by now,' remarked Shani. 'Especially since elephants really like being together.'

Jake knew what Shani meant. Whenever he saw a herd of elephants, he was struck by just how close and affectionate they seemed. So it was really strange that Goliath preferred to be on his own.

Goliath stopped sweeping his trunk across the ground. He stood still, staring down towards Jake and Shani, his face heavy with disappointment.

'Sorry,' Jake said. 'But we're only doing what's best for you.' He ducked behind a shrub. 'Let's watch him from here for a while,' he whispered to Shani who crouched down next to him.

They peeped out between the leaves. Goliath paced briskly along the fence, looking very frustrated that they had disappeared. Jake expected him to turn and head back into the bush, but suddenly he lifted his trunk and trumpeted loudly, shattering the peace of Musabi. Then he leaned one sturdy shoulder against the fence and pushed with all his might.

'Crumbs!' Jake gasped, as the fence bent like a sapling under Goliath's weight. 'What does he think he's doing?'

'It's like he's mad at us for leaving him,' said Shani.

'Or for not giving him any bananas,' Jake suggested.

Goliath pushed harder. Jake held his breath, convinced the elephant was about to push the fence right over. But to his relief, Goliath soon spied another target for his anger – a tall fever tree growing nearby. The elephant spun round and reached the tree with a few giant strides. He dug his tusks into the trunk and stripped the sulphur-green bark away in long shreds, leaving a gaping bare patch down one side.

'Wow!' Jake whistled softly as Goliath shook the strips of bark off his tusks then slammed his forehead into the tree and pushed until it began to buckle. The fever tree swayed back and forth, creaking under the strain.

'Maybe he knows we're still here,' suggested Shani. 'So he's trying to get our attention.'

'OK. Let's leave,' Jake said. 'In case he starts tearing down the fence!'

They slipped out from their hiding place and started back across the lawn. Glancing back, Jake saw Goliath had stopped ramming the tree. He stared after Jake and Shani while slowly flapping his huge, Africa-shaped ears.

Shani shaded her eyes and looked through the fence at a sparkling water hole about two hundred metres away. 'He must be hot. You'd think he'd go for a swim.'

'I wonder why he doesn't,' Jake said, his green eyes squinting against the sun as he looked at a herd of zebras and several impala standing in the slimy grey mud at the water's edge. 'Perhaps it's too crowded for him.'

Suddenly Shani nudged Jake with her elbow. 'Hey! There's another elephant. And it's huge.'

Jake saw a big adult with long curved tusks emerging from the thick bush on one side of the pool. Close behind it came several other elephants. Most of them were adults, but there were also a few very young calves trotting along next to their mothers.

Jake glanced at Goliath. The solitary young bull stood tensely watching the other elephants. There was a curious look on his face – an expression of longing, Jake thought. 'Just look at him,' he said to Shani. 'I bet he'd love to join in really.'

It reminded Jake of the first days at his new school in Dar es Salaam, a few months ago. Coming from a school in Oxford, England, Jake had felt a bit strange at first, as if he didn't really belong. But at least he'd had a friend to help him settle in. Like Jake, Shani was a weekly boarder and as she lived in the nearby village of Sibiti, the two had met before term started.

Suddenly, down at the water hole, the mood changed as the elephants left the water and crowded together on the bank, bumping against one another and trumpeting noisily.

'What's going on?' Jake wondered. He ran over to the fence and ducked behind a tree so that Goliath wouldn't see him.

'Maybe they've seen a lion,' suggested Shani, crouching down next to Jake.

Jake caught his breath. It was thrilling to know that there were lions in Musabi, but he had mixed feelings about them being so close to his house!

Especially after he'd recently seen the full rage of a lioness who was trying to get to a pair of cubs that were being used to make a movie in the reserve.

But it wasn't a lion that was causing the excitement right now. It was another elephant arriving at the drinking hole, a massive animal that stood head and shoulders above the matriarch who had started walking towards him, as if she was going to greet him.

'Wow!' Jake gasped. The elephant had the biggest tusks Jake had ever seen.

'Magnificent, eh?' said a deep voice behind Jake.

'Uncle Morgan!' exclaimed Shani, turning round. 'I didn't hear you arrive.'

Morgan Rafiki was Rick's right-hand man on the reserve, a tall athletic man with gentle brown eyes. 'I'm not surprised you didn't hear my footsteps, with all that racket going on over there,' he said.

'What's going on?' Jake asked, looking back at the restless herd. 'Is the big one a long lost relative or something?'

Morgan smiled. 'Not exactly. You see, that tusker there is known as *Mlima* – it means mountain in Swahili. He's the biggest bull in Musabi. He's been in the south of the reserve for a few months, which is why you haven't seen him before.'

'What's he doing here now?' said Shani.

'Looking for a new wife,' Morgan explained. 'And it looks like he's found one.'

Mlima and the matriarch stood facing each other, their trunks intertwined above their heads, while around them, the rest of the herd kept up their noisy jostling.

'It looks like they're all at a wedding!' laughed Shani.

'That's a good way of putting it,' her uncle grinned. 'Elephants always celebrate a new love affair in the herd.'

The celebration at the water hole just made Jake even more aware how lonely Goliath looked. 'What's wrong with Goliath?' he asked Morgan.

Shani's uncle shrugged. 'I wish I knew,' he said. 'He's been here long enough to team up with a herd. But something is stopping him.'

'Like what?' Shani looked concerned.

Morgan shook his head. 'Who knows? Something in his past, perhaps.'

'Before he went to Rungwa?' Jake suggested.

'That's my guess,' answered Morgan. 'He's unusually anti-social, and I don't think that's just because he was raised by humans. I think something very traumatic must have happened to him. Something that is still troubling him.'

Almost as if to confirm Morgan's guess, Goliath suddenly uttered a deep rumbling sound. He flapped his ears a few more times, then turned and vanished into the trees.

TWO

'Anyone want to come with me to Rungwa for a couple of days?' Rick asked casually at supper that night as he opened a bottle of wine and poured out two glasses.

'You bet!' Jake said. 'When are you going?'

'Tomorrow morning,' Rick told him, passing a glass of wine to Jake's mum, Hannah. 'Don McClaren rang up this afternoon to ask if I'd help him design a new enclosure for rescued cheetahs.'

Rick was a well-known authority on big cats. Before coming to Tanzania five years ago, he'd worked with lions and tigers at London Zoo. 'When I told Don that you and Shani were home for the half-term holiday, he said you were welcome to come along too,' Rick explained.

'Cool,' said Shani, her brown eyes sparkling. Shani's home was normally in Sibiti where her mum

– a nurse and midwife – ran the clinic, but she was spending part of the October half-term holiday at Musabi.

Jake felt a soft, damp nose nuzzling his shin under the table. It was Bina, his tame orphaned dik-dik. Jake and Rick had rescued the miniature antelope after her mother was taken by an eagle. Sneaking a piece of cucumber off his plate, Jake slipped it to Bina. He wasn't really supposed to feed her at the table, but he had missed her during the first half of term, and couldn't resist letting her follow him into the dining-room. He was about to filch a lettuce leaf for her when he caught his mum's eye. She was leaning back in her chair, watching him with a look of amusement on her face.

To take her mind off the illicit feeding session under the table, Jake said, 'Are you coming to Rungwa too, Mum?'

'I'd really like to,' Hannah said. 'But unfortunately I've got a deadline to meet at the end of next week.' Hannah Berman was a wildlife journalist and photographer. She grinned at Jake, her blue eyes twinkling. 'And anyway, someone's got to stay here and look after that bundle of mischief under your chair.'

Jake grinned back guiltily, then picked up his knife

and fork and tucked in to his dinner again while trying to ignore Bina, who was now nibbling his ankles.

'What's your article about?' Shani asked Hannah. 'More chimps?'

Just recently Hannah had published a hard-hitting article on the capture of baby chimps for the illegal pet market. This was after she and Jake had visited a chimpanzee sanctuary in neighbouring Uganda and experienced at first hand the inhuman trade in endangered primates.

'No. This time, I'm dealing with dung beetles,' Hannah told her.

Shani was about to take a bite of a bread roll. 'Yuck!' she grimaced, putting the roll down. 'Dung beetles! Why did you pick them?'

Hannah laughed. 'Because they're fascinating in lots of ways. Some of them are dung thieves who steal other beetles' dung balls and use them as their own, for example. And there are tens of thousands of different species.'

'*Tens of thousands!*' Jake echoed in amazement.

'That's right,' Hannah nodded. 'The world's full of them. It's just as well too – they do a very important job of burying dung that would otherwise just lie around for years.'

'Yep! Where there's dung, there's beetles – and nowadays, wildlife photographers,' grinned Rick.

Jake, Shani and Rick set out for Rungwa just before dawn the next morning. The sanctuary was in the south of Tanzania, about four hours' drive from Musabi and not far from the Zambian border.

The hour before the sun rose was Jake's favourite time to drive through the bush. There was always a good chance of spotting animals like leopards, porcupines, bushbabies and servals returning to their daytime hideouts after a night of hunting. Jake kept his eyes peeled for any movements as they rattled over the cattle grid at the end of the bumpy driveway, then headed along the dirt road through the game reserve.

They hadn't gone far when they found their way blocked by a fallen tree. Rick stopped the Land Rover and they all jumped out.

'Careful,' Rick warned Jake and Shani. 'It's a thorn tree.'

'I know,' grimaced Jake, feeling a needle-sharp spine stab him in the arm as he slid his hands under the trunk and started heaving the tree off the road. Even though it was a small tree, it was surprisingly heavy. Jake wondered what had made it fall, then, in the beam of the Land Rover's headlamps, he noticed that most of the bark had been stripped from the trunk. 'Hey!' he exclaimed, recalling how Goliath had de-barked the fever tree the day before. 'I bet an elephant pushed this over.'

'More than likely,' Rick agreed.

'It could have chosen something less prickly to block the road,' Shani grumbled, dropping the branch she was holding with a crash and sucking her finger where a thorn had pierced her skin.

'An elephant's hide is so thick, he probably doesn't even notice the thorns,' puffed Rick, as they hauled the tree off the road then shoved it into a shallow ditch next to a termite mound.

'Here's your breakfast,' Jake laughed, tapping the side of the ant-heap, then he swung himself back up into the front seat of the Land Rover next to Shani.

Glancing back over his shoulder, Jake's gaze was drawn to the top of a craggy slope behind the termite mound. There, framed by the first rays of the sun, was the dark bulk of a single elephant. As Jake watched, he lifted his head and trumpeted loudly, as if to wake up all of Musabi.

The sound sent a shiver down Jake's spine. 'It's Goliath,' he said, spotting the right-angled tusk silhouetted against the brightening sky.

Goliath trumpeted again then dropped his trunk and stood motionless, a lonely figure on top of a hill, staring down at the reserve like a stone sentinel.

Later that day, the two friends and Rick were in a hide at Rungwa with the McClarens, the Tanzanian couple who owned the sanctuary. The reed and thatch shelter overlooked a water hole where two young bull elephants were play-fighting. Five other elephants were wallowing in the pool, the smaller ones almost completely submerged.

'I wish Goliath would learn to mix with other elephants, like this,' Jake remarked.

'Wouldn't that be brilliant?' agreed Shani.

Don McClaren had explained that all seven elephants had been rescued, either from snares or after their mothers were killed by ivory poachers. The sanctuary owner smiled at Jake when he expressed concerns about Goliath's loneliness. 'Don't worry. Goliath's still a youngster, and young bulls often roam about on their own until they join up with a bachelor herd.'

'But he doesn't show any interest in the other elephants at Musabi. It's like he doesn't even recognize that they're the same as him,' Jake argued. 'He'd rather hang around humans.'

'Well, he always did like people more than most elephants do,' Don admitted. 'I remember him trailing after us most of the time when he first came here.'

'And in those days, we had the time to indulge him and give him lots of attention because we didn't have a lot of other animals to look after. In fact, Goliath was the first elephant we took in,' said Don's wife, Anita. In contrast to her burly, tanned husband, Anita was slim and elegant and wore a large-brimmed hat to keep the sun off her fair-skinned face. 'If I remember correctly, he was about three when the next elephant arrived.'

Don and Anita had once farmed cattle at Rungwa, but it wasn't long before the ranch became more famous as a place where orphaned or injured wild animals could be sent. Eventually, Don and Anita had decided to sell their cattle and turn Rungwa into a proper sanctuary.

'Perhaps we shouldn't have made such a fuss of Goliath,' Anita went on. 'But it was hard not to. He was only about six months old when he came here, and very traumatized. Don even had to spend the first few nights sleeping in the shed with him.'

Don's face creased into a broad grin. 'The first and last time I'll volunteer to be a matriarch,' he chuckled, his dark brown eyes glinting. 'I was up all night feeding him.'

'So who looks after the orphans now?' asked Shani, watching one of the calves trot over to an older female and lean his trunk against one of her front legs as if he wanted some motherly attention.

'We still do it ourselves occasionally, but we've also employed local men to act as keepers,' explained Anita. 'Come on. Let's go back to the compound and you can meet our keepers, Wilson and Herbert – and Sugar and Spice, our two newest elephants.'

They retraced their footsteps along the fenced-in path that led from the hide to where the Rungwa jeep was parked. Don and Anita generally drove around the sanctuary because, although not as big as Musabi, Rungwa was still about fifty hectares in size.

The residential compound stood in the middle of the sanctuary. It was made up of the McClaren's thatched house, several wooden barns and a number of large enclosures where animals were kept until they could be released with the other rescued animals.

Jake and Shani peered through the slatted wooden fence that surrounded one of the enclosures.

'I think it's empty,' Jake began, but then he glimpsed two spotted tails sticking out from behind a bush. 'Cheetahs!' he exclaimed with a thrill. He'd only seen a few of the beautiful lithe cats before, and usually at a distance.

'They're brothers, and only a few months old,' said Anita, coming to stand next to Jake. 'Their mother was shot on a cattle ranch nearby. The farmer insisted she was a threat to his livestock, but we have our doubts about that.'

'Unfortunately, some people see a big cat and immediately assume it spells trouble,' Don explained. 'So their first reaction is to kill the animal.'

A second enclosure contained some animals that Jake had never seen before. They looked like skinny mongrel dogs with patchy black and yellow coats. 'What are these?' Jake asked Anita.

'Oh, those are very special,' Anita answered with a broad smile. 'They're Cape Hunting Dogs.'

'*Mbwa mwitu*,' added Shani. 'The wild dogs of Africa.'

Jake was impressed. 'Have you see them before, then?'

Shani shook her head. 'No. But we learned about them at school last year. Our teacher said they're very rare.'

'Dangerously rare,' put in Rick. 'They're on the brink of extinction thanks to farmers who have persecuted them for decades.'

Jake studied the four dogs. They were staring suspiciously at the fence, their large, rounded ears twitching as they listened to the humans talking outside. 'Do we have any at Musabi?' he asked Rick.

'Yes. A pack of about twenty,' said Rick.

Jake grinned at his stepdad with delight. 'Can we track them next time we go on a bushwalk?'

'We can try,' Rick smiled as they followed Anita and Don to one of the barns. 'But I doubt we'll have much luck. They're very elusive. I've only seen the Musabi pack a few times myself.'

Anita pushed the barn door open. Inside, it was cool and airy, with the distinctive gamey smell of elephants.

'There they are,' announced Don, taking off his sunglasses and pointing towards a far corner. 'Sugar and Spice.'

Jake could just make out a pair of tiny elephant calves standing in deep straw. With them were two men in khaki uniforms.

'*Jambo*, Wilson and Herbert,' said Don, going over to them. 'How are our little ones today?'

'Very well,' said one of the keepers.

Don introduced Jake, Rick and Shani to the two men. 'Rick's going to help us design the new cheetah enclosure,' he explained.

'That's good,' Wilson nodded. He looked at Shani and Jake. 'Would you like to help us take the *tembos* for a walk? It'll be their first time out since they came to Rungwa.'

'Cool,' breathed Shani, her face lighting up. She walked over to the elephants. At about a metre tall, they stood as high as her shoulders, and their sturdy round bodies almost swamped her slim frame.

'They're really strong now, but they weren't when they first came here,' Anita told them. 'We even thought we might lose Sugar, she was so weak and dehydrated.'

'What happened to them?' asked Shani.

'Oh, the usual,' said Don in a weary tone. 'Their mothers were shot for their tusks. Rangers from a nearby game park found the calves next to their mothers' bodies after they'd been dead for a couple of days.'

'What about the rest of the herd?' asked Rick, frowning. He took off his hat and ran one hand through his thick blond hair.

'No one knows what happened to them,' said Anita. 'Probably caught in snares some time earlier and removed by the poachers.'

'What kind of snares?' Jake put in, surprised that

23

an animal as big and powerful as an elephant could be caught like this.

'Just ordinary wire loops – the type that an animal steps into. When it tries to pull its foot free, the snare tightens, eventually cutting deep into the flesh,' Rick explained. 'Once that happens, there's no way the animal can escape. It dies from thirst and starvation, unless the poacher returns first and shoots it.'

'That's dreadful,' Jake said with feeling.

'At least these two were lucky,' said Don, rubbing Spice's broad head. 'Another few hours, and they'd have died too.'

Watching Sugar and Spice, Jake thought how different things had been for Goliath all those years ago. Even though the young bull had been rescued and cared for just like them, he'd never had the chance to be part of a real herd. And now, as he reached adolescence, it looked as if he'd never fit in with his own kind. He was set to live alone for the rest of his life.

THREE

'Ready to go walkabout?' Jake said to Sugar. In reply, the little elephant heaved herself on to her feet then leaned her trunk against Jake's leg, in the same way the calf at the water hole had leaned against the older elephant earlier that day.

Herbert laughed. 'She's treating you like her mother.'

Jake couldn't help feeling flattered. He rubbed Sugar's head and smoothed her wrinkly cheeks. Enjoying the attention, Sugar lifted her trunk and started puffing hot breaths of air into Jake's face.

'OK. That'll do. Enough of this mother and baby stuff now,' Jake chuckled, pulling his face away.

'What happens now?' Shani asked Wilson. 'Do you have to put leads and harnesses on them?'

Wilson shook his head. 'No, they'll follow us,' he answered. 'Just like they'd follow their herd in the wild.' He walked across to the barn door and opened it. 'Come on, everyone,' he said. 'Let's go.'

Just as Wilson had said, Sugar and Spice padded obediently after their substitute herd to the narrow door. They kept close to Jake and Shani, as if they'd decided to adopt them as their keepers for the time being.

At the door, Shani stepped aside to let Jake and Sugar go through first. 'Lead the way, *Mama Tembo*,' she said to him.

Wilson and Herbert roared with laughter.

'*Mama Tembo*,' Wilson repeated under his breath, his dark, handsome face creased in a wide grin.

Outside, the baby elephants blinked and looked around at the bush that stretched away on all sides.

'They look a bit dazed,' Jake said. He stroked Sugar's head. The calf pressed herself closer to him while Spice wound his trunk around Shani's arm.

'Maybe they're scared to be out in the open again after everything that's happened to them,' Shani suggested.

'Maybe,' agreed Wilson. 'But they'll relax soon enough, you'll see.'

They set off down a well-worn path leading away from the compound. Sugar and Spice walked along next to Jake and Shani, their trunks swaying comfortably from side to side. At first the calves walked so slowly that Jake had to adjust his speed to make sure he didn't go too far ahead of Sugar. But after a while, the elephants grew more confident and their hesitant walk changed to a loping trot. Jake soon found himself trotting too. 'Hey! I thought we were going for a *walk*,' he puffed.

Behind him, he heard the keepers laughing. 'You're the one who is setting the pace,' one of them called to him. 'Just slow down.'

Jake stopped running, and was relieved to see Sugar matching his speed. He looked back at Shani and Spice. Shani had picked a branch off a tree and was offering it to the calf. Spice sniffed at it then curled his trunk around it and carried it along like a stiff little flag, looking very proud of himself.

The dusty path petered out at a small water hole. Turtledoves strutted about on the muddy banks, their gentle cooing the only sound in the still afternoon.

Herbert bent down at the edge of the pool and scooped up a handful of water. 'Here, Spice,' he said, holding his cupped hand at the bottom of the calf's trunk. 'Have a taste.'

But Spice seemed to have other things on his mind. He was watching the turtledoves pecking in the mud just a few trunk lengths away. One of them was walking towards him, its head nodding back and forth as it scouted for food. Spice stared at the bird, then without any warning, charged towards it.

'Hey! It's only a bird,' Shani called, running after Spice.

The little bull stormed across the mud, his trunk swaying wildly, his thin tail raised, and his ears spread wide. The doves looked up at him in alarm. They took off with a noisy flapping of wings and flew to the other side of the pool.

'Too bad!' Jake laughed, as Spice skidded to a halt and watched the birds land out of reach. 'Better luck next time.'

Shani looked puzzled. 'Why did he go after them?' she asked Herbert. 'Elephants aren't predators.'

'He's just playing,' Herbert told her. 'Baby elephants love chasing birds.'

'But he's also learning to charge,' Wilson added as Spice turned round and trotted back to them. 'One day, when he's older, he'll run like that when something threatens him. Sugar will too.' He patted the young female who was dipping her trunk into the water. 'Especially when she has a calf of her own. Elephants can get very angry if they think their babies are in danger.'

Sugar siphoned up some water but instead of curling her trunk into her mouth to drink, she pointed it straight at Jake and sprayed him with a muddy stream.

'Hey!' Jake exclaimed, wiping his face. 'You're not supposed to do that to your elders!'

Herbert clapped his hands and laughed loudly. 'Maybe *Mama Tembo* should teach the daughter some manners.'

Wilson reached across and tenderly ran his hand over the folds and creases on Sugar's face. 'She was only testing her trunk. And the older elephants will discipline her when she joins the herd.'

The shadows were lengthening when they finally started back for the compound. The calves seemed tired, and happy to leave the water hole and go back to their barn.

They were nearly at the end of the path when a loud trumpeting broke out from further away in the bush. The effect on the calves was electric. They stopped dead and spread out their ears, listening with every fibre of their body. And then, Jake heard the pair utter a strange, deep rumbling. It was so low that it was more of a vibration than a sound, like distant thunder rolling across the plains.

'What's going on?' Jake whispered to Herbert.

'They're calling to the other elephants,' answered the keeper.

'But it's such a low noise, even I can hardly hear it,' Jake frowned. 'How can the others pick that up?'

'Oh, they hear it,' Herbert assured him. 'It's the way elephants talk to each other over long distances.'

'I wonder what they're saying?' asked Shani.

Jake stared at Sugar. Suddenly she seemed different, more confident and less clingy, as if hearing the call of her own kind had reminded her of what she was and where she'd come from. 'Perhaps they're telling the others to wait for them,' he said, half expecting the calves to go charging towards the direction of the noise.

But Sugar and Spice didn't move. Instead, they fell silent again and stared intently into the bush.

'It looks like they're listening to the others rumbling back to them,' suggested Shani.

'Or they're making even deeper noises,' said Wilson. 'You see, sometimes we can't even hear the rumbles, they're so low.'

'How do you know that if you can't hear them?' Jake queried.

Wilson smiled. 'Before I came to Rungwa I worked with a scientist from America. She had a special machine that could pick up very low sounds. She called it infrasound.'

Jake looked closely at Sugar and Spice. Their eyes were half closed as if they were concentrating hard on something. Were they calling out silently to the herd in the distance, or listening to the equally soundless reply?

Picturing Goliath, Jake remembered the times he'd seen the young bull gazing into the distance with a faraway expression in his eyes. 'Hey!' he said, a welcome thought coming to him. 'Goliath can use infrasound, too.'

'So?' said Shani, looking puzzled.

'Well, maybe he *does* have contact with other elephants in Musabi after all,' Jake insisted. 'We just can't hear what he hears.'

'OK. Suppose he hears them,' reasoned Shani. 'That doesn't mean he answers back.'

Jake knew that Shani had a point.

Suddenly, Sugar and Spice relaxed and turned back to Jake and Shani, their inquisitive trunks once more prodding their clothes and arms.

'Is the conversation over?' Jake murmured, stroking Sugar's trunk. 'Are you ready to come home with us now?

Back at the barn, Jake and Shani helped to feed

Sugar and Spice, then returned to the house where the delicious smell of dinner greeted them.

'Mmm! Smells like *bizari*,' said Shani as they walked through to the patio where they'd had lunch.

'*Bizari*?' Jake echoed. 'That sounds . . . er, *bizarre*! What is it?'

'Curry,' Shanti told him. 'And I hope it's a really hot one.'

'Well, I don't,' Jake admitted. He was still trying to get used to the ultra-spicy food that was popular in Tanzania.

The McClarens and Rick were sitting on the patio enjoying sundowners. Don pulled out a couple of folding canvas chairs for Jake and Shani. 'Had a good walk?' he asked.

'Brilliant,' Jake said. 'Sugar and Spice kind of met up with some other elephants.' He described the elephants' long distance conversation.

'Isn't it just fantastic how they keep in touch like that?' said Anita. She poured a cold drink each for Jake and Shani and passed them a bowl of salted macadamia nuts.

Rick leaned back in his deck chair and stretched out his long legs. 'They're certainly very complex animals,' he agreed.

Don nodded. 'And the way things are going, we'll

probably never fully understand them either.'

'Is that because they're endangered?' Jake asked.

'That's right,' replied Don. 'And not just the elephants. One day, man will be piecing together sun-bleached bones to see what an elephant, or a rhino, or any of a hundred other species looked like.'

'Like they do with dinosaur bones,' suggested Shani.

'Exactly the same,' said Don.

Jake thought this was a rather gloomy outlook. 'But there are lots of people working to conserve these animals,' he reminded Don. 'Like Rick, and you and Anita, and all the other people in charge of game reserves.'

'That's true,' Anita smiled kindly. 'But—' She was interrupted by the telephone. 'Back in a minute,' she said, getting up and going inside.

She reappeared carrying a cordless receiver. 'I think you'd better deal with this, Don,' she said, giving it to him. 'It's Mark Cooper, the vet from Lufubu.'

'Lufubu?' Rick echoed as Don took the phone. 'That's a private game reserve in Zambia, isn't it?'

'Yes. It's just across the border,' said Anita. 'Mark says they're in a critical situation with some of their elephants. They keep breaking out of the reserve and causing havoc in a nearby village.'

'You mean destroying crops, wrecking homes, fences and the like,' said Rick.

'That sort of thing,' Anita nodded. She turned to Jake. 'This kind of clash between humans and elephants is exactly what I was going to tell you about before the phone rang. You see, these villagers are subsistence farmers who can just about feed their families on the crops they manage to grow. So it's really hard on them when an elephant herd invades their land and ruins everything.'

'It's a very scary thing,' said Shani sympathetically, and Jake wondered if her village had ever been threatened in this way.

He tried to imagine what it must be like having a whole herd of elephants going on the rampage outside his house. 'And we've got a solid home,' he murmured. 'Not a mud hut that an elephant could easily squash.'

Don was listening intently to the vet on the other end of the phone. Every now and then, Jake heard him make a comment, or ask a question such as, 'How many in all?' or 'What about the water supply, Mark?'

Eventually, Don said, 'I don't know if there's a lot we can do to help.'

Jake wondered what kind of help the vet was

hoping to get. After all, what could be done to stop elephants from going wherever they wanted?

With a deep sigh, Don answered Jake's unspoken question by saying, 'I'm sorry, Mark. We just don't have the room to take in a full herd. We're jam-packed here ourselves.' He paused again and listened, then said, 'Look, just put things on hold for a day or so, if you can, Mark. We'll get down there tomorrow morning to have a look. Rick Berman from Musabi is with us. He might be willing to come along too.' He gave Rick a questioning look and received a nod of agreement. 'OK. It's settled,' said Don. 'We'll be there around eight o'clock, I guess.' He paused, then added slowly. 'But you could be right, Mark. Culling might be the only answer.'

FOUR

Culling! Jake nearly fell off his chair with shock. This was the last thing he'd expected to hear. Less than five minutes ago, Don had been saying how elephants were in danger of dying out completely – bleached bones and all that – and now he was agreeing that a herd of them might have to be killed. 'Aren't the elephants supposed to be protected in Lufubu?' Jake burst out as Don put down the phone.

'That's the general idea,' replied Don. 'But we have to balance the needs of the elephants with the needs of their human neighbours. And the only answer in this situation might be to destroy the ones that are breaking out.' He stood up and poured himself another beer then went to the edge of the patio and gazed across the grasslands that stretched before him. 'You see there are just too many elephants in

Lufubu,' he went on, 'and that's largely because there are too many humans.'

Jake glanced at Shani. She was looking as puzzled as he felt. 'But I thought it was because of too many humans that the elephants were threatened,' Jake said.

'Precisely,' said Don.

Jake was more confused than ever. 'What do you mean?' he asked.

Don came back to his chair. He sat down and leaned forward, his elbows resting on his knees. 'Once, the elephants – in fact all the wildlife – roamed freely across Africa. For thousands of years, they followed ancient migration routes in search of food and water. But the human population explosion that started just over a century ago has changed that forever. More people means more development and less wilderness.' He paused to take a sip of beer then went on. 'The early European settlers also had a big impact on the land. They cleared huge tracts to establish farms. So the wildlife was pushed back even further until they ended up in isolated sanctuaries. You can think of game reserves as islands, if you like. Islands surrounded by oceans of people.'

'At least they're safe there,' Shani pointed out.

'You mean, they *should* be safe,' Jake put in. He still couldn't see the point of having a game reserve, then culling the very animals the place was set up to protect.

'They're safe to a degree,' explained Rick. 'But only if the reserve can sustain their numbers.'

'You mean, as long as there's enough food and water for them?' said Jake.

'That's right,' Anita nodded. 'And with the elephants protected in one place, their numbers grow until you get a situation like the one that's developed at Lufubu. They're just too crowded there. And because they eat so much, they have to start looking for food elsewhere. Like the farms on the boundaries of the reserve.'

Jake was beginning to understand why Don said it was so complicated. 'So they're just trying to do what their ancestors did,' he said. 'Migrate to other places searching for food.'

'Which is very difficult because people have settled on their traditional migration routes,' Don reminded him. 'And that's where you get the clash between animals and humans.'

'So no one really wins,' Shani concluded sadly.

'That's right,' said Anita, gathering up the empty glasses and going inside.

'And I always thought that ivory poachers were the elephants' biggest threat,' Jake said, thinking of Sugar and Spice whose mothers had been killed for their tusks.

'Poachers have certainly done a lot of damage,' Rick agreed. 'But they're just part of the wider problem caused by mankind.'

Anita came back out carrying a tray laden with bowls of steaming curry and rice. She put the tray down on the long wooden dining table that was set for dinner. 'Here, please help yourselves.'

They took their places at the table. Jake looked at the curry. Even though he was very hungry, he couldn't help wishing there was something to eat that wouldn't burn the roof of his mouth! And then he thought of the farmers labouring all year to grow crops, only to have them destroyed by elephants who, in turn, were struggling to survive on a limited supply of food. Suddenly Jake felt almost guilty at how lucky he was, and ladled a heap of the spicy food on to his plate.

Jake perched on the edge of his seat for much of the journey to Lufubu in Zambia the next morning. He kept wondering what they'd find when they arrived. What if the elephants had been on the rampage again during the night? And, worse still, what if some people had been hurt? He thought back to when Goliath had shaken him off the fence the other day. Jake had come to no harm, but it could have been a lot worse if Goliath had really meant business!

At Lufubu, Mark Cooper was waiting for them at the reserve's main gate. 'Thanks for coming so quickly,' he called as Don pulled up next to the vet's jeep. 'The situation's just about out of hand here.'

Jake saw Shani's eyes grow wide. 'Have the elephants been out raiding again?' she asked, scrambling out of the vehicle.

'No. Not last night,' Mark reassured her. 'But it's only a matter of time before they do break out again. If we don't sort this out soon, someone's going to get killed.' He turned and pushed open the back door behind him. 'Climb in,' he said to them. 'I'll take you to see the herd.'

Jake climbed in to the back of Mark's jeep with Rick and Shani, while Don sat in front.

'I hope "sorting it out" doesn't mean the elephants will end up being killed,' Jake whispered to Shani as Mark started up the engine. During the journey from Rungwa that morning, Rick and Don had explained that in some game reserves, elephant numbers had grown so much that the area could no longer support them all. The local wildlife department might then carry out a 'problem animal control' programme; in other words, a regulated cull of the elephants. Jake had felt his blood run cold at the thought, but Don had pointed out that if the elephants were left unchecked, their eating habits would eventually destroy the reserve. 'And that spells the end for all the species there, including the elephants themselves. It's what we call a population crash,' Don had said.

But even though Jake could now see the sense in limiting the numbers of elephants, he still thought it was a terrible irony that endangered animals had to be killed to ensure the survival of their species. He was relieved that this wouldn't happen at Musabi which, Rick had told him, was about twenty times bigger than Lufubu.

Mark drove along a narrow dirt road that led west across a wide plain. The land was flat so Jake could see for a long way all around. He was struck by how sparse the vegetation was in this part of Lufubu. Everywhere, trees lay uprooted on their sides, while others that were still standing had been stripped completely of their leaves and bark, leaving shiny naked trunks. Beneath the trees, the ground was hard and bare, resembling the dusty football field in the village of Sibiti where Shani lived. With a jolt, Jake realized that there was almost nothing left for the herbivores to eat. 'They must have hundreds of elephants here to have done all this,' he said to Rick.

'Yes. Just look what they did to that baobab,' said Shani, pointing to the massive tree which had almost been turned to pulp by the elephants.

'Actually, there aren't that many elephants here,' said Mark over his shoulder. 'Only about fifty. But when you think that adults feed for fourteen hours a day and eat more than a hundred kilograms of food each, then you can see how a small reserve like Lufubu can quickly turn to dust. The place never gets a chance to recover.'

After a few kilometres, Mark turned off the road and parked at a viewing point which overlooked a dry river bed. 'I saw them here earlier,' he said, as they climbed out of the jeep. Mark walked away from the jeep, his boots crunching across the stony ground. He was thin and very tall, and, like Don and Rick, deeply tanned from working in the sun. Scars criss-crossed his legs and arms, and one ran all the way from below his left knee to his ankle, an angry red line with dots either side showing where the skin had been stitched back together.

'Something must have gored him pretty badly,' Shani whispered to Jake, who had been thinking the same thing.

Mark stopped at the edge of the viewing area where the land fell away steeply to a dried up river below. He pointed to the other side of the dusty river bed. 'There's the herd, under those fig trees.'

'They don't look all that menacing,' Jake commented, looking through his binoculars. The herd was nothing like the restless, angry group he had pictured. Instead, they looked calm and relaxed as they rested in the shade. There were about ten elephants in all, including a couple of tiny ones that lay on their sides on the dusty ground, surrounded by the tree-trunk-like legs of the adults.

Jake trained his binoculars on the bigger elephants, trying to decide which one was the matriarch. A large, powerful-looking individual with two very straight tusks caught his eye. 'Is that the leader?' he asked Mark, pointing.

'No. That's one of her sisters,' Mark answered. 'You're looking for Rosa, the one at the back. She's the one who's responsible for all the trouble.'

Jake peered at Rosa through his binoculars,

adjusting the focus until she appeared with stark clarity. He drew in his breath sharply. Compared to her sister, Rosa looked worn out, even weak. Her backbone and hips stuck out like a toast-rack, and her head drooped, as if it was too heavy for her to hold up. 'Is she OK?' he asked hesitantly.

'Oh yes. She's a tough old girl,' said Mark.

'She doesn't look very tough,' protested Shani, lowering her own binoculars. 'She looks *feeble*!'

'That's partly because she's out of condition from not having enough food. You've seen what the vegetation is like around here – there isn't any,' Mark said. 'But Rosa is suffering more than the rest of the herd because her youngest daughter was killed last week, and she's grieving, just like a human mother.'

'Poachers, I assume,' Rick said gloomily.

'Uh-huh,' Don joined in. 'We caught a gang a couple of months back, but another lot quickly took their place.'

Shani was fidgeting with her bead bracelet – a sign that something was troubling her. Jake braced himself for what she was about to say, and wasn't disappointed.

'What's the difference between you culling

elephants and poachers shooting them?' she demanded. 'You're both *killing* them.'

Mark gave her a sad smile. 'Indeed,' he said. 'But there's a whole different level of pain in killing just one or two members of a close-knit family, as a poacher would. Elephants are deeply social animals and care enormously for one another.'

'You mean they *love* each other?' asked Shani, frowning.

'As far as animals can love, yes,' said Mark. 'And they certainly grieve when one of them dies. Just look at Rosa.'

Jake focussed his binoculars on Rosa's face again. Her wrinkled skin and drooping eyelids made her look utterly miserable. She dropped her trunk and dabbed at the ground, puffing up small dust clouds as she looked for something to eat. Standing slightly apart from the others, she seemed to be locked in lonely sorrow. This made Jake think of Goliath and how, according to Morgan, something way back in his past must have led to him being so anti-social. 'I wonder how long Rosa will grieve?' Jake murmured.

'Maybe for ever,' suggested Shani. 'You know that people say elephants never forget.'

Jake nodded. 'It must be true,' he said, still thinking of Goliath.

One of the babies was waking up. It rolled over and tried to get up but toppled on its side again in the dust. This jolted Rosa into action. She stretched out her trunk and helped to steady the tiny calf as it struggled to its feet. When the baby had made it on to all fours, it trotted over to the big female that Jake had mistaken as the matriarch and began to suckle. Rosa ambled slowly after it, then stood a few paces away, watching it feed.

Seeing this, Jake changed his mind about Rosa being as isolated as Goliath. At least she belonged to a herd. He lowered his binoculars and turned to Mark. 'I see what you mean,' he said. 'Elephants really do care for each other.'

'Those two don't!' said Shani, as two smallish adults at the edge of the herd started pushing and shoving each other with their trunks.

'It's nothing too serious,' laughed Mark. 'They're just sparring – perfectly normal behaviour in adolescent bulls, testing their strength. They'll be leaving the herd soon, either voluntarily or when the females drive them off, to join up with other young bulls.'

'Like Goliath was supposed to,' Jake nodded.

They studied Rosa's herd for several minutes before Mark said, 'Seen enough here?'

'I reckon so,' Don replied.

'OK. Then let's go and see the chaos they've caused,' said Mark, striding back to the jeep. 'I'll first show you where they're getting through the fence,' he said, starting up the engine, 'and then we'll go to the village.'

They drove for fifteen minutes with Jake leaning out of the side window, eager to see just how Rosa and her herd had broken out of Lufubu. He imagined an elephant-sized gap in the fence where the group had managed to slip through, so when he first glimpsed their escape route, he was shocked. The elephants had completely demolished a stretch of the strong wire barrier several metres long. It lay in a tangled heap on the ground amid several sturdy posts that had been knocked down like skittles.

'What did they do? All charge it at once?' Jake gasped.

'It looks like it,' agreed Mark, turning off the road and driving across the rough, stony ground towards a team of workers who were repairing the fence. In their bright blue overalls, the men stood out clearly against the bare brown landscape. 'But it's not nearly as dramatic as that,' Mark went on. 'Rosa just pushes the wire down with her trunk then the rest of the herd steps over it quite easily.'

'Like it's made of chicken wire,' Shani commented.

'Pretty much,' said Mark, stopping the jeep next to the workers' truck.

Jake realized what a lucky escape he'd had when Goliath had grabbed the Musabi fence the other day and shaken it like a toy. *I could have ended up mangled like that wire!* he thought, a shiver running down his spine. He forced the uncomfortable thought to the back of his mind, then climbed out of the jeep and looked around.

Inside Lufubu it was like a desert, but just a few hundred metres outside the fence, trees and bushes grew in thick dark green clumps. It must have been more than the elephants could stand.

'No wonder Rosa's crowd broke out,' Jake said. 'It's much more inviting out there.'

'It won't be for much longer if they keep getting out,' Shani reminded him grimly as they walked over to the workmen whose overalls bore the Lufubu logo of an eagle with outstretched wings.

'Everything OK?' Mark called to the perspiring men.

'Yes – just as long as the elephants don't come back before we finish here,' said one man. He wiped his forearm across his face then, with straining muscles, lifted up a section of the strong wire and tried to straighten it.

Rick strode forward to help. Taking his cue from his stepdad, Jake joined in. They pulled the mesh up between them, gradually uncrumpling it. When it was more or less straight, they held it still while the man fixed it to a steel post that another man had driven into the ground.

'I guess Lufubu doesn't have the funds to electrify the fence?' Rick called over his shoulder to Mark who was helping to reposition another post in the ground.

'You guess right,' responded Mark. 'And even if we could afford to, the electricity supply is so erratic out here that most of the time there isn't any!'

'Pity,' remarked Don, heaving a heavy branch off an area of the fence that, although buckled out of shape, was still standing.

Shani was helping Rick and Don to pull up another stretch of wire. 'An electric fence,' she echoed in a disapproving tone. 'That's dangerous. Someone could get killed if they touched it by mistake.' She stepped away and dusted off her hands as the worker nailed the wire to the post.

Rick smiled at Shani. 'Not really,' he assured her. 'The voltage would only be enough to give a nasty shock.'

'Unfortunately, though, these fences don't deal with the basic problem of too many elephants, not enough vegetation and now, no water,' said Mark, coming over to them.

'Are you having a drought here?' Jake asked, thinking about the dry river bed where Rosa's herd had congregated. 'Or is it your dry season?'

'A bit of both,' answered Mark. 'It is the dry season, but normally the river keeps flowing which provides the elephants with enough water until the rains start again.' He paused and looked towards the farmlands. In a low voice edged with frustration, he continued, 'But this year, there's very little water in the reserve because the farmers have diverted the river to irrigate their crops.'

Don frowned. 'That's a big problem,' he said. 'You'll never keep the elephants in if they've got no water. What about creating a few artificial water holes?' he suggested as they turned to go back to the jeep.

'We've thought of that,' said Mark, swinging open the driver's door. 'And we've sunk a borehole in the north. But we're still left with the problem of the elephants eating anything that's green.' He shrugged his shoulders. 'Let's face it. The elephants have just outgrown Lufubu.'

'I'm afraid you're right,' agreed Don. 'And there aren't a lot of options left.'

This was the last thing Jake had wanted to hear, even though he'd now seen for himself how desperate things were in Lufubu. *Goliath's so much better off than these elephants*, he told himself. *He may be lonely, but at least he's got plenty of food and water*.

In a sombre mood, they followed a dirt track running next to the fence, then left the reserve through a gate and headed down a narrow road towards the farms. From a distance, Jake could just make out the cleared land and behind it, on a gently sloping hill, the village where the farmers and their families lived. It looked a lot smaller than Sibiti. Looking through his binoculars, Jake counted twenty-two houses, most of them made from mud and thatch, while a few sturdier ones were built with concrete blocks and had flat tin roofs that glinted in the sun. Chickens scratched about in the stony ground surrounding the houses, and Jake noticed a woman sitting under a tree using a stone to grind grain. Nearby, several children played in the rusty remains of an ancient car.

Mark drove along the road beside some fallow farmland, keeping parallel with the Lufubu fence. After a while he stopped the jeep near what, at a casual glance, looked to Jake like a ploughed field.

But when he looked closer, he realized just how wrong he was. Far from being prepared for planting, the field had been completely churned up, its crop of vegetables destroyed. All that was left were a few cabbage leaves that lay half-covered by soil.

In a neighbouring field, an entire crop of maize had been flattened, and the wooden fence designed to keep out livestock had been smashed to smithereens. Jake thought it looked as if a tornado had hit the area. 'The elephants did all *that*?' he exclaimed, staring appalled out of his window.

'That and more,' said Mark heavily, opening his door. 'Come and see.'

They left the jeep and followed Mark through the fields, picking their way round the crater-like holes left by the elephants' massive feet. After a while the ground became damper, then very muddy.

Jake was puzzled. Everywhere else was so dry. 'Where did all this mud come from?' he asked.

'It used to be a series of trenches that diverted water from the river to the fields,' Mark explained. 'But the elephants came here to drink and all the embankments collapsed.'

'So now the water floods the surrounding land before it even reaches the crops,' Rick observed. He pushed his hands into his trouser pockets and shook his head. 'You can't really blame the elephants. But I can understand how angry the farmers must be.'

Jake looked up at the little settlement. It was about two hundred metres away, just above the ruined maize field. He noticed some pumpkins put to ripen on top of the tin roofs. *Just as well the elephants didn't see those*, Jake thought grimly, imagining Rosa flattening the huts to get at the plump orange fruit.

A small crowd had gathered in front of one of the huts. They were watching the visitors examining the destroyed fields. A man stepped out from the crowd then, beckoning the others on, headed down the hill. 'Mr Cooper,' he called out, waving to him when he was in earshot. 'We must talk to you.'

'This isn't going to be easy,' Mark said in a resigned voice. 'That's Stanley Chibembe, the headman. He wants an immediate answer to the problem.'

'And you haven't got one for him,' Rick put in.

Mark nodded just as Mr Chibembe came up to him. The two men politely shook hands while the villagers clustered around them and started to speak very quickly in a language Jake couldn't understand.

'We're doing all we can . . .' Mark began, but he couldn't make himself heard above the noise of the crowd.

Mr Chibembe raised one hand to hush his villagers, then he said to Mark, 'You know the elephants have gone too far this time—'

But before he could finish, another man pushed in front of him. He brandished a stick in the air. 'If the elephants come back we will kill them!' he threatened. Behind him another angry villager spoke up loudly, 'We will call the ivory hunters to help us.'

Jake stared at the people in alarm. 'I hope they don't really mean that,' he whispered to Shani.

'They do mean it,' she replied. 'Look how thin they are.' She pointed to a toddler whose belly swelled out in front of him. 'That's not a fat tummy,' she said. 'It's bloated like that because he's got *kwashiorkor*.'

'What's that?' Jake asked.

'It's a disease children get when they don't have enough good food,' Shani explained simply.

Jake didn't know what to say. The people were starving, the elephants were starving, and the land just couldn't support them all.

Mark tried again to reassure the villagers. 'Please don't take matters into your own hands,' he said. 'It could be very dangerous.'

Don went to stand next to Mark. He gestured to Rick. 'My name is Don McClaren. My friend, Rick Berman, and I have come from Tanzania to see if we can find a way to stop the elephants from breaking out.'

'We'll work as fast as we can to find the answer,' promised Rick. 'But it may take us some time.'

'We haven't got time,' shouted the man with the stick. He pointed to the ruined crops in the trampled fields. 'What can we eat now?'

'We'll do what we can to help,' Mark promised. 'I have ordered bags of maize to be delivered later this week. And we will help you to repair the water furrows. But in the meantime, we ask you to be patient.'

'Patient!' echoed a wizened old woman. She was impossibly thin, with hollow cheeks and sunken eyes. Leaning on a stick, she hobbled out from the jostling crowd which parted respectfully and fell silent as she walked forward. 'You ask us to be patient when we have no food for our children any more. How can patience fill their bellies? How can patience stop their tears when they have to go to bed hungry? How can patience help the little one standing in the way of the elephants? Our children must be protected. And we will do whatever we have to.'

Behind her, the villagers cheered. And in that moment, Jake recognized in the old woman a matriarch determined to lead her people to safety – just like Rosa leading her family to food and water. Neither intended any harm to others. They just wanted to protect their families.

FIVE

'It's hopeless,' Jake said gloomily to Shani.

They were standing behind Rick, Don and Mark, listening anxiously to the heated exchange.

'I know. Someone's going to have to back down,' Shani replied, fidgeting nervously with her bracelet.

'And I guess that will have to be the elephants,' murmured Jake, the word *cull* echoing again and again in his mind.

Don turned to look at him. 'I'm afraid you're right, Jake. There's not much hope for Rosa's herd. With just an ordinary fence between them and the fields, they'll keep breaking out to find food and water.'

'Isn't there *anything* you can do?' pleaded Shani, going to stand next to Mark. 'Like move the elephants to another part of Lufubu?'

'That won't make any difference,' said Mark. 'They'll find their way back here in no time at all.'

He took off his sunglasses and rubbed his eyes. He looked exhausted. 'Basically, we've run out of options,' he continued. 'We've exceeded our carrying capacity here at Lufubu, the elephants are desperate for water, and if Rungwa's full there's nowhere else for the elephants to go. The only thing left is to cull the herd as quickly and as humanely as possible.'

There it was. *Cull*. The word Jake had been dreading. This wasn't how it was supposed to end. He bit his lip and looked away, catching Shani's eye as he did. Even though she understood what things were like for the farmers and villagers, she looked as upset as he was by Mark's announcement.

But for others, Mark's decision came as a lifeline. The old woman had been listening carefully to Mark and Don. Now, she turned to face her people, and in a shrill, reedy voice, told them in their own language what Mark had said. A sigh of relief ran through the crowd. The crone hobbled over to Mark and grasped his hand. 'Thank you,' she said in a low, earnest voice. 'We have been so worried. Now we will be able to sleep at night.'

Mark shook her hand, but said nothing.

Gradually, the villagers started to disperse, some going back to the village, and others to the fields to see what crops they could salvage. One or two stopped to exchange a few words with Mark. 'It's a pity there is no other way,' said one farmer, his face heavy with sadness. 'Elephants are wonderful creatures. But against them, we have no chance.'

Mark nodded. 'I know,' he agreed, then added soberly, 'And against mankind, the elephants have little chance, too.' As the farmer walked away, Mark took off his cap and ran a hand through his thinning blond hair. 'I guess all that's left now is for us to plan the cull,' he said. 'I'm sorry to have brought you all the way down here for nothing. The problem is really Lufubu's. It's not as if there's much you could do to help us.'

Rick looked thoughtful. 'Maybe there is,' he murmured.

'What do you mean?' Jake frowned, hardly daring to hope that Rick had a better solution to the problem than culling the elephants.

'I reckon we could consider translocating Rosa's herd,' Rick went on, as they headed back to the jeep.

Jake's heart sank with disappointment. Rick must have forgotten what Mark had said earlier about moving the elephants to a different place in the reserve.

Shani had been thinking the same thing. 'But Mark said it wouldn't make any difference if the herd was moved to the other side of Lufubu,' she put in, walking alongside Rick.

'That's not what I'm talking about,' said Rick.

'You can't mean Rungwa,' said Don, glancing over his shoulder at Rick who was just behind him. 'As I told Mark last night, we're full to bursting. There's no way we can take in Rosa's herd.'

'I know,' Rick nodded. They came to the jeep and Rick opened one of the back doors. 'But *we* can.'

Jake was just behind him. 'Us!' he exclaimed, spinning round to look at Shani. He could hardly believe what he'd just heard. Shani looked equally surprised. 'Are you serious?' Jake went on. 'You want to move Rosa's herd to Musabi?'

'That's right,' Rick confirmed, stamping his feet to loosen the mud that was caked on his boots.

'But Musabi's hundreds of kilometres away,' Jake pointed out. 'How would you get them all the way there?'

'With a lot of effort,' said Rick. 'But it's not impossible.' He looked at Mark who was leaning against the bonnet of the jeep, listening intently. 'We're nowhere near our carrying capacity at Musabi. We have only about eighty elephants at present, and plenty of vegetation and water. So I reckon we could easily accommodate Rosa's small herd.'

Jake was speechless with amazement, while the vet looked as if the weight of the world had been removed from his shoulders. 'That's the best thing anyone's told me in days,' Mark declared.

'Sounds good to me,' smiled Don from inside the jeep.

Jake found his voice again. 'It's a brilliant plan!' he said. He could just see Rosa leading her herd through the bush at Musabi. It was the perfect place for them. They'd be totally safe there and with the rich food supply, they'd never even think of breaking out. 'When do we move them?' he asked Rick eagerly.

'Hold your horses, Jake,' cautioned his stepdad. 'I said we can accommodate them easily. But that's the only easy part. Translocating elephants can be very tricky. It's not something we undertake lightly at all.'

'That's right,' Don agreed. 'It's a huge upheaval for the herd to be moved from their home range to an unfamiliar territory. In a way, it's the ultimate interference by man.'

'But it's better than culling them,' said Shani.

'It is, as long as everything goes smoothly,' Don replied. 'And sometimes some of the elephants refuse to settle in their new home. Once, we translocated a small herd to Rungwa from an overstocked reserve about a hundred kilometres away, and they broke out immediately and found their way back.'

'What happened to them then?' Jake asked.

Don gave him a strange look. 'I think you can work that out for yourself,' he said in a low voice.

Jake refused to think about things going wrong. *It will be different with Rosa's herd*, he told himself.

The others were getting into the Land Rover. Jake climbed into the back next to Rick and shut the door. 'What does translocation actually involve?' he asked as Mark set off down the road towards Lufubu. In England, Jake had seen cattle and other livestock being transported in big trucks, but these were domestic animals that were used to humans. Moving a herd of wild African elephants had to be a whole different ball game.

'A helicopter, tranquillizer darts, antidotes, transport trucks, a team of skilled helpers,' Rick listed. 'And considerable danger,' he added seriously.

Jake felt a rush of excitement. This was something he just *had* to see. But Rick's next words brought him back to earth with a bump.

'And that's only part of the story,' his stepdad warned. He looked at Shani who was staring out of her window with a worried expression on her face.

'We have to consider the people living outside Musabi, in villages like Sibiti.' He gestured to the ruined crops and churned up fields behind them. 'The last thing we need is a situation like this. So don't worry, Shani,' he said with a smile, putting a hand on her shoulder. 'Before I can make a final decision, I'll need to talk to the local people on our boundaries. We have to make sure that the elephants won't be a threat to them or their farms.'

'And how do you do that?' Jake asked. Having seen for himself just how much damage the elephants could do, he knew that if he was one of the villagers living near Musabi, he wouldn't be all that keen to have them so close to his land.

'Well, we can do our best to make sure the elephants can't get out. And that means making the fence a lot stronger than it is now. Even electrifying it where it runs close to villages,' Rick explained. 'Luckily, we have wealthy sponsors who will fund projects like that.'

'But that'll take ages,' Jake protested, all too aware that time was fast running out for Rosa's herd.

'We'll need a few days,' Rick admitted. 'Do you think you're going to be able to keep the herd in for a bit longer, Mark?'

The vet looked at Rick in the rear-view mirror and

raised his eyebrows. 'With Rosa in charge, that's easier said than done. But we'll patrol the fence around the clock, and do our best to drive the elephants back if they come anywhere near the boundary.'

'That sounds great,' said Rick. 'I'll give you a call as soon as I know if we can definitely take them.'

Jake looked at Shani. She smiled back at him, her troubled expression fading. 'Keep your fingers crossed,' Jake urged. 'We *must* help Rosa and her family.'

Two days later, Rick and Morgan met with the people of Sibiti to discuss bringing Rosa's herd to Musabi. The meeting took place in the school hall, and by the time the Bermans, Shani and Morgan arrived, the small room was already jam-packed.

'It looks like the whole village is here,' Jake whispered to Shani as they squashed up behind Rick and Hannah on the tiny platform. Already, it was hot and sticky in the hall, and Jake was perspiring as if he'd run all the way there from Musabi.

'Just about the whole village,' agreed Shani, looking around the room. 'And there are even people from other places.' She pointed to four men leaning against the wall in one corner. 'Like those over there. They're definitely not from Sibiti.'

'News travels fast around here,' Jake remarked.

'It's the bush telegraph,' chuckled Shani.

More and more people arrived, until latecomers had to listen outside at the open windows, or crowd around the door. The people talked to each other in loud, excited voices which only fuelled Jake's fears that the meeting would end in disaster, the villagers completely against the plan to bring Rosa's herd to Musabi.

Rick was about to start the meeting when there was a disturbance at the door.

Jake craned his neck to see what was going on. 'It's Mr Gorongo,' he told Shani, as the crowd shuffled noisily aside to let the portly man through. 'Why's he pushing in like that?'

Julius Gorongo owned Sibiti Trading Store, the only shop in the village. Jake really liked the jovial, friendly man but today he looked quite different. His usually laughing face was set in a serious frown, and he walked solemnly up to the stage, holding a stout cane in one hand.

Shani laughed softly. 'Don't you know?' she said. 'He's our chief.'

'Your chief?' Jake repeated. 'You mean, like the mayor of Sibiti?'

Shani wrinkled up her nose. 'Mayor?' she echoed,

looking puzzled. 'Does that mean like a father to everyone in the village?'

'Er, not really,' said Jake, thinking of the mayor he had seen in Oxford, wearing robes and a heavy gold chain.

'Well then, Mr Gorongo's not a mayor,' said Shani.

There was no more time for her to explain. The chief mounted the wooden steps to the stage then sat down on the rickety chair that Morgan had saved for him. Rick nodded to Mr Gorongo who lifted his hand in a formal gesture and said, 'OK, Mr Berman. You can proceed.'

Speaking in English, Rick outlined his plan to bring Rosa and her herd to Musabi. He paused every now and then so that Morgan could translate his words into Swahili for those who couldn't understand English.

The villagers listened intently, but even before Rick had finished talking, they broke into an uproar. Jake could hear some angry comments in English, like, 'More elephants? Never!' and, 'Musabi has enough. Why do we need more?'

Jake slumped in his chair. Just as he'd feared, the people were dead against the move. What hope was there for Rosa's herd now?

Rick put up his hands. 'Please listen,' he urged

them. He started to explain how he intended to make the fence stronger, and even electrify it for about fifteen kilometres, but it was impossible to make himself heard above the agitated chatter of the crowd.

Suddenly, Julius Gorongo stood up and banged his cane on the floor. 'Quiet everyone,' he commanded in such a loud voice that the room fell instantly silent.

Jake sat up straight again.

'We must discuss this in a calm way,' the chief went on firmly. He turned to Morgan. 'Please tell the people what Mr Berman has just said.'

Morgan repeated what Rick had said about the fence, but many of the farmers were still not convinced. Those who objected most of all were the village elders who could remember a time many years before when elephants regularly raided their crops.

'But that was before Musabi was made into a game reserve,' Morgan reminded them. 'Then the elephants were free to come and go. Now, they have to stay inside Musabi.'

Jake was sure this would be enough to satisfy the elders, but Julius himself put forward another argument.

'These Lufubu elephants are used to getting out,' the store-keeping chief began in his deep, rumbling voice. 'If you bring them here, will they not just do it again?'

Enthusiastic shouts came from the floor of, '*Ndiyo*! Yes! Chief Gorongo speaks the truth. We'll lose all of our crops, just like they did at Lufubu.'

Jake sighed with frustration. 'Julius has really scuppered things now,' he muttered.

Shani shot him a glance. Her brown eyes were filled with concern so that Jake assumed she agreed with him. But he was wrong.

'We can't have elephants trampling our homes and fields,' she told him.

'But Rick's already promised us that won't happen,' Jake argued. 'You heard him say that there's enough food inside the reserve for them. And anyway, they won't get through the fence.'

'We don't know that for sure,' Shani insisted. 'What if they break out where it isn't electrified?'

Jake had no answer to this. He slumped down in his chair again, feeling a deep gloom overtake him as the protests grew louder in the hall. With public opinion so strongly against the elephants – both at Musabi and Lufubu – it looked as if Rosa and her herd were as good as culled.

But Rick hadn't given up yet. He held up both hands to quell the raised voices. 'I promise you, the elephants won't get out of Musabi,' he said. 'We're different from Lufubu. You see, we have very few elephants, so there's more than enough food for them here. They won't need to go in search of more.'

Julius contemplated this silently for a few seconds, before speaking again. 'But like the people said, we already have elephants in Musabi. Why bring more?'

For the first time since the meeting started, Hannah spoke up. 'Because it will benefit us all,' she said. She leaned across and put one hand on Morgan's arm. 'Tell the people how more wildlife will encourage more tourists to come here,' she urged him. 'If people know they'll definitely see elephants here, they'll flock to Musabi. And that will mean more opportunities for all of us.'

'What kind of opportunities?' Jake asked his mum, feeling a surge of hope.

'For starters, more jobs,' explained Hannah. 'We'd need to employ more people to act as tour guides, or to help maintain the camps, or to work in the office.'

'And that's not all,' said Morgan. He pointed to the pretty handmade basket on Hannah's lap, containing her sunglasses, purse, keys and hat. Morgan's wife had made the basket and given it to

Hannah as a gift when she first arrived at Musabi. 'Our people will be able to sell a lot more crafts and curios,' said Shani's uncle.

'There's other work, too,' put in Rick. 'We'll need teams of men to help us with the fence.'

The stern expression on Julius's face was slowly relaxing. 'Even my shop might get busier,' he mused. He banged his cane on the floor again. 'People of Sibiti,' he announced. 'Rick Berman promises the elephants will not roam outside Musabi. But there is more. They will bring us good fortune.'

The crowd stared up at him in surprise and Julius went on to explain the benefits of increasing Musabi's elephant population.

Jake felt the mood of the crowd changing. Eventually, one of the village elders spoke up. 'We are ready to welcome the elephants. But first we must know that the fence on this side of the reserve is strong.'

'Agreed,' said Rick. 'We will start work on it first thing in the morning. We'll need to employ people to help us, so those of you looking for work, please give your names to Morgan.'

A number of men, including the strangers in the back corner, started to make their way through the crowd. But Jake squeezed past Shani and made sure he was first in the queue. 'Count me in,' he told his dad's right-hand man.

'Sure,' said Morgan with a broad smile. 'But for you there's no pay. You're too young to be employed.'

'That's OK,' Jake said. As far as he was concerned, there *would* be a handsome reward – the chance to be involved in translocating the elephants, and releasing them into Musabi.

SIX

Jake uncoiled a length of electric cable and passed one end up to Morgan. Shani's uncle was standing on a ladder so that he could reach the top of a tall fence post. Behind him, the farmers' lands stretched away towards the horizon, the maize, cabbage and wheat crops flourishing after the early rains.

'Thanks,' said Morgan, fixing the strand to an insulator on top of the pole. He called across to Shani. 'Please bring me the big pair of pliers from my toolbox.'

It was early the next day, and already the fence was well on the way to becoming elephant-proof, with several parallel strands of special wire added to the existing barrier, ready to be electrified. Buckled sections were also being torn down and replaced with strong new panels. Morgan, Jake and Shani had driven to the site at dawn to find the villagers who had signed up for the job already there, eager to start work. Jake was hugely relieved to see them. He'd hardly slept, worrying that the people would change their minds overnight and refuse to allow the project to go ahead.

Morgan quickly organized the workers into four teams, then allocated them to work on different sections of the fence. In all, fifteen kilometres had to be repaired and electrified before Rosa's herd arrived.

For many of the people, the elephants were already making a difference. 'I will put some of the money away for my son's education,' Jake overheard one man telling a fellow worker, while another said he could now afford to fix the roof of his house. 'The chief was right,' said a woman who was helping her husband to uncoil a roll of strong wire mesh. She looked round and flashed a smile at Jake. 'The elephants are bringing us good luck.'

'Very good luck,' agreed one of the strangers Shani had pointed out at the meeting the day before. He was a very dark, thin man with an angular pock-marked face. He'd told them his name was Kenneth and that he and his companions, Tebogo, Abdi and Joseph, had come a long way looking for work. They'd brought tents with them and asked Morgan if they could set up camp just inside Musabi while they were working on the fence. Morgan warned them about the dangerous wildlife in the reserve, but the men were quite untroubled, saying they were used to the bush and would keep a fire burning all night as a precaution.

It was soon apparent to everyone that the four were skilled at fencing, unlike most of the locals who had little experience in this type of work. Delighted to have such handy men on board, Morgan assigned each of them to head up a team.

'They're really helping to speed things up,' Morgan remarked to Jake, watching Kenneth swiftly hammer a new fence panel to a post, then beckon his team to follow him to the next section that needed repairing.

'At this rate, we'll be able to go back for Rosa's herd really soon,' Jake said.

'Let's hope so,' Morgan responded. He climbed back down the ladder and picked up one end. 'Help me carry this to the next pole please, Jake. And Shani, you can bring my toolbox over.'

At lunchtime, the workers downed their tools then sat in the shade and tucked into the food they'd brought with them.

Jake opened his backpack and took out two big

packs of sandwiches he and Shani had made before they set off that morning. 'Peanut butter or honey?' he said to Shani.

'Both, please,' answered Shani, taking a sandwich from each pack. 'I'm starving.'

'Just as well we made so many,' Jake smiled, helping himself too. He leaned back against the trunk of a Mopane tree. A yellow-billed kite landed in the tree and peered down at Jake, its beady eyes fixed on his sandwich.

'Forget it,' Jake grinned. 'This is my lunch. You can find your own.'

A few metres away, under another Mopane tree, the four strangers were taking turns to drink water from a plastic Coke bottle. Jake noticed they didn't have anything to eat. 'Let's give them some of our food,' he said to Shani.

'Good idea,' she agreed.

They went across to the men and offered them some sandwiches.

'*Asanteni*,' Kenneth thanked them as he took one. 'We've run out of food and were waiting to earn some money to buy more.'

No wonder they're all so thin, Jake thought with a pang of sympathy. *It's lucky they happened to arrive in Sibiti when this work came up.*

'Where do you come from?' Shani asked the men.

'From the north,' replied Abdi.

'Yes. Near, er . . . Serengeti,' put in Joseph.

Jake had heard of Serengeti. It was a famous game reserve near the border between Tanzania and Kenya. 'Have you been there?' he asked eagerly. Rick had promised to take him next time the whole family had a holiday.

'Oh, many times,' came Kenneth's reply. 'It is an exciting place. With so many animals. Plenty of rhinos and elephants.'

'I can't wait to go there,' Jake said, passing the men a bag of macadamia nuts.

'Oh, but you have a wonderful place here,' said Kenneth. 'With much game too.' He took a handful of nuts then, leaning forward with an earnest expression on his face, asked, 'How many elephants is your father bringing to Musabi?'

'About ten,' Jake told him.

'And how many are here already?' said Kenneth.

'Um, about eighty, my dad said,' Jake answered.

'Have you seen the big one with the long, long tusks?' Tebogo asked. 'The one they call Mlima?'

'You've heard of Mlima?' Shani sounded surprised.

'Oh yes,' smiled Tebogo. 'He's a legend.'

'Is he really?' Jake was flattered to think that such a famous animal lived in Musabi. 'I suppose I never thought elephants could be famous outside their own reserves,' he said. He grinned at Shani. 'Isn't it cool to think of people sitting round a campfire and talking about our elephants as far away as the Serengeti?'

Kenneth was still leaning forward, his expression even more intense. 'Tell me about Mlima,' he said earnestly to Jake. 'Is he really so big?'

'He's *huge*,' Jake confirmed. 'His tusks must be at least two metres long!'

'Two metres!' Kenneth echoed. 'I must try to see this elephant.'

His companions nodded in agreement. 'Perhaps we'll be lucky and he'll come near our camp one day,' said Abdi.

'You must be crazy!' exclaimed Shani. 'I wouldn't want such a big elephant anywhere near my tent. I'd be scared to death.'

The men smiled at her. 'Oh, he wouldn't harm us,' one assured her.

Over by the fence, Morgan was calling everyone back to work. The four men stood up and dusted their hands on the seats of their trousers. They thanked Jake and Shani for sharing their lunch with them, then strode back to join the work gangs.

'That's funny,' remarked Shani, watching them go.

'What is?' Jake looked curiously at her.

'I thought they were poor,' said Shani.

'They are,' Jake insisted. 'After all, they said they had no money to buy food.'

'But Kenneth has a mobile phone,' Shani pointed out, frowning. 'I saw it on his belt when he stood up.'

'A phone doesn't mean that someone's rich,' Jake argued. He looped the straps of his backpack over a branch of the Mopane tree to keep it out of reach of ants. 'Lots of ordinary people have them these days. Maybe he bought it the last time he had some money, and he just uses it for emergencies.'

'I guess so,' agreed Shani. She bent down to tie a loose shoe lace then, straightening up again, sighed, 'Back to work.'

The two of them returned to Morgan who was already unrolling the next strand of electric wire that would run along the bottom of the fence.

By mid-afternoon, the teams had made good progress. Digging a deep hole for a new metal post, Jake paused and looked towards Sibiti. The village was about a kilometre away on the other side of the fence. *The people are going to be safer than ever when the fence is finished,* he mused.

Morgan saw Jake leaning on his spade. 'Tired?' he asked him.

'No,' Jake said, and to prove it, quickly drove his spade into the earth again.

Morgan smiled. 'Well, I am. So we'll just finish sinking this post then take a short break.'

With sweat pouring down his face, Jake finished digging, then stood back to let Morgan put the new post in the ground. It fell into the hole with a satisfying thud and Morgan hammered it in firmly with a heavy wooden mallet. 'OK. That'll do,' he puffed. He beckoned to a man who was mixing concrete with a spade. 'You can fill in the hole now,' he told him. 'Jake and Shani, you keep holding the post upright.'

The man shovelled some of the wet mixture into a wheelbarrow then trundled it over to where Jake and Shani were standing. He was about to start filling the hole when he gasped loudly, dropping his shovel with a clatter. *'Tembo mkubwa!'* he croaked, staring into the bush behind Jake, his eyes like saucers.

'Big elephant? Where?' Jake spun round.

No more than fifty metres away, partly hidden by a baobab tree, stood the mighty Mlima, a look of intense curiosity on his broad, wrinkled face.

'The legend of Musabi,' Shani whispered while all

around, the workers froze in shocked silence.

Even next to the massive baobab tree, the bull elephant looked colossal. Jake thought he had to be at least double Goliath's height, and maybe three times his weight. And as for his tusks – at this close distance they looked as lethal as the sharpest sword!

The air bristled with tension and no one dared even to whisper as people waited fearfully to see what the huge elephant would do. *He's just being curious. He won't harm us,* Jake tried to convince himself, but at the back of his mind, he could hear Rick's stern warning about the unpredictable nature of wild animals.

In turn, Mlima kept up his unblinking gaze, as if he, too, was waiting to see what would happen. He spread out his ears and waved them slowly.

Jake saw that one of Mlima's ears was very ragged, with several holes near the edges. He wondered if they could be bullet holes, but dismissed the thought almost immediately, guessing that the harsh life in the bush was probably responsible for the damage. He was pretty sure that poachers didn't operate in Musabi.

Mlima took a few paces forward. Shani sucked in her breath and Jake marvelled at just how quiet the elephant was. His legs were as thick as a tree trunk yet when his enormous round feet struck the ground, there wasn't even a thud. *How is that possible?* Jake wondered, thinking how hard he found it to walk quietly through the bush.

As he padded down towards them, the elephant's heavy trunk swung rhythmically from side to side so that it almost slammed into a pair of white egrets pecking on the ground. The startled birds scurried out of reach, then flew up and landed on his back as if they'd decided to hitch a lift. One of them strutted forward and stood between Mlima's ears. The huge bull shook his head to dislodge the bird, which took off into the air for a moment before landing back on Mlima's head.

The elephant ignored the egret. He walked on, his gaze still fixed on the humans in front of him.

Jake's mouth went dry. A few more steps and Mlima would be right among the work party. He stopped again, dabbed at the ground with his trunk, then swung it up and with a mighty *whoosh* blew a shower of red dust all over himself. The egrets flapped noisily away to escape the dust bath, and landed at the top of the baobab tree.

Despite the danger of standing just metres from an adult bull elephant, Jake nearly burst out laughing. Mlima's action had seemed almost deliberate, although Jake was sure it was just a coincidence. Rick had explained to Jake that elephants regularly gave themselves dust baths to protect their skins against insect bites.

Covered in a thin layer of red dirt, Mlima kept up his steely gaze. Then, quite suddenly, he turned round and loped away into the bush. As silently as he had appeared, the huge grey giant vanished.

'Phew! That was scary,' Shani whispered.

Gradually, the villagers started to relax and find their voices. They seemed more concerned with the threat Mlima posed than their good fortune to see the famous elephant.

'This fence will never hold back a huge elephant like that,' complained one farmer. 'Once he sees my maize, he'll break through easily to get it.'

'And on top of that, Mr Berman is bringing known crop raiders into this reserve,' muttered another man. 'So with them and the big one, I don't know why we're bothering with this fence.'

Morgan quickly tried to reassure the men. 'Trust me, the elephants won't get through an electric fence.'

To Jake's surprise, Kenneth backed up Morgan. 'Mr Rafiki is right. Electricity is one of the few things that will stop an elephant,' he said. He beamed at his three companions. 'What an elephant!' he exclaimed. 'One of the best. We were lucky to see him.'

Jake felt warmed by Kenneth's enthusiasm for the amazing animal. It was a nice contrast to the pessimistic response from the local people. But, Jake realized, Kenneth and his companions didn't live here, so they didn't have to worry about the elephants trampling their homes and fields. Even with the electric fence, it still didn't look as if Rosa's family was going to get a warm reception from the Sibiti villagers.

At half past four, Morgan paid everyone for the day's work and people started heading back to the village. A few remained behind to help Morgan prepare for the next day, in exchange for a lift home later. They lived on small farms on the outskirts of Sibiti, a few kilometres further along the perimeter fence.

The four northerners pocketed their wages then set off in the direction of their camp. Jake overheard them telling Morgan that they had settled on a site at the foot of a rocky ledge not far away. They'd even found a small cave which offered them better protection than their canvas tents.

'I bet it's fun, sleeping in a cave in the wild,' Jake

said enviously to Shani as he tossed some strands of leftover wire into a cardboard box.

'Yes, but only if there's a strong gate at the entrance,' Shani joked. 'Listen.' She put a finger to her lips.

Jake listened. He could hear a deep booming *du du dududu* – the call of a ground hornbill, a large black turkey-like bird with red fleshy growths on its head and throat. There were other sounds too – the chirps and squawks of other birds preparing to roost for the night; the short, sharp bark of baboons; the high-pitched excited bark of zebras, and the eerie *whoop* of hyenas. And as an ominous backdrop to all of these, was the rumbling bass roar of a pride of lions deep within Musabi.

'OK, Shani. I get your point,' Jake grinned.

Shani picked up a broken plastic transformer and tossed it into the box, then she peered into the long grass at her feet. 'Hey! Look here. A mobile phone. I bet it belongs to that man from Serengeti. He must have dropped it.'

'We'd better see if we can find the camp and give it to him,' Jake said.

They went over to Morgan and told him where they were going.

'You're not going into the bush alone,' said Morgan. 'I'll come with you.'

'But the men said their camp is really close,' Jake protested. 'We'll only be a few minutes.'

'I don't care,' said Morgan sternly, then repeated, 'You're not going alone. And anyway, I know exactly where the cave is. In fact, you two wait here. I'll return the phone.'

Jake felt a pang of irritation. In his opinion, adults could sometimes be a bit overprotective.

'But we want to see the cave,' Shani pleaded. 'We've never been to that part of the reserve.'

Morgan frowned at her.

'Please!' implored Shani.

Morgan gave in with a shake of his head. 'OK. But stay close to me.' He signalled to the remaining workers that he'd be back shortly. 'You can wait in the Land Rover if you're worried Mlima will come back,' he told them.

The workers didn't need a second invitation. They picked up their belongings and were in the vehicle in a flash.

'I guess it's easier to be relaxed if you carry a gun,' chuckled Morgan, shouldering his rifle and setting off in the direction the four men had gone.

'But you'd never shoot unless you had to, would you?' Jake asked.

'Only if a life was in danger,' Morgan assured him.

They picked their way through the long grass, keeping an eye open for Mlima, or any other animals that might suddenly appear. Not far from the work site, the terrain changed dramatically. The open savannah gave way to dense bushes, thick copses of trees, and a steep cliff rising up on one side of a narrow river.

'Be on the alert,' Morgan said to Jake and Shani. 'This is rhino and buffalo territory.'

His warning couldn't have come at a better time. Just ahead of them, a powerful black rhino came crashing through the bushes. In a flash, Morgan slipped his rifle off his shoulder but the rhino suddenly veered away, weaving through the trees like a football player dodging his opponents. Jake drew in a shaky breath, his legs like jelly.

'See what I mean?' said Morgan, glancing back at Jake and Shani.

Shani made a small strangled sound that might have been a yes, while Jake could only nod. Maybe Morgan wasn't being too protective after all.

The smell of fire soon told them that they were near the men's camp. Through the trees, Jake saw a thin trail of smoke rising up in front of a craggy rock face. Narrowing his eyes, he spotted the four men crouching down near a bush, some distance from the fire. They seemed to be examining something on the ground.

'Hello there,' Morgan called out.

The men looked round at once, apparently startled.

'It's only us. We've brought your phone,' Jake said loudly to reassure them.

His announcement seemed to have the opposite effect, however. The men scrambled to their feet and fled deeper into the bush, crashing recklessly through the trees until they were out of sight.

'What's going on?' Jake exclaimed, floored by their reaction.

'They must be hiding something,' said Morgan grimly. 'Let's see what it is.'

But before they'd gone very far, an ear-shattering trumpeting filled the air.

'Elephant,' Shani gasped.

The chilling cry came again, louder than before. It sounded terrifyingly close. Seconds later, the four men came running back towards their camp, fear written all over their faces. One stumbled and fell, almost landing in the fire, then scrambled up just as an elephant came charging out of the bushes behind them, its ears spread wide and its trunk raised in anger.

'It's Goliath!' Jake yelled, spotting the elephant's distinctive right-angled tusk.

The young bull's angry cry echoed in Jake's ears as he plunged through the camp, trampling the fire underfoot.

Suddenly one of the men stopped and whipped round to face Goliath. And in that instant, Jake's blood ran cold. The man held a double-barrelled hunting rifle. 'No!' Jake shouted.

But his voice was swallowed up by the deafening gun blast that shattered the air.

SEVEN

For a moment, time stood still. Nothing moved as the gunshot reverberated off the rocks. Goliath and the four northerners stood frozen like statues.

Jake waited helplessly for Goliath to slump to the ground. The gun had been aimed straight at him. He must have been hit on the head, perhaps even between the eyes.

But amazingly, Goliath stayed on his feet, a smouldering mixture of anger and shock on his broad face. Then he lifted his head, and with a trumpeting shriek broke the silence that gripped the bush.

Time kicked in once more. The four men spun round and sprinted into the bush; Goliath, clearly unhurt, turned and loped back the way he'd come, and Jake finally understood what had happened. 'The man didn't shoot. It was *you*!' he exclaimed to

Morgan who was gripping his rifle in both hands, the barrel pointing upwards.

Morgan's harmless warning shot had stopped Goliath and the men in their tracks. Jake's head reeled as he realized that if Shani's uncle hadn't pulled the trigger, either the men or Goliath would almost certainly have been killed.

But there was no time to discuss what might have happened. Morgan was already going after the men. 'Keep up with me,' he yelled to Jake and Shani.

Running as fast as they could over the rocky ground, they pursued the four men who, thanks to their head start, were already clambering up the cliff face just past the campsite.

Jake, a natural sprinter, reached the bottom of the cliff ahead of Shani and Morgan and began hauling his way up the slippery rocks. But he was barely a third of the way up when the men disappeared over the top.

'It's no good. We'll never catch them now,' Morgan called up to him.

'Yes, we will,' Jake called back.

'No, we won't.' Morgan sounded grim as he sat down on a boulder to rest. 'Men like these know how to hide in the bush.'

Jake jumped down to the ground. 'What on earth are they up to?' he asked Morgan.

'Whatever it is, it's no good,' Morgan answered. He stood up. 'Come. Let's see what they've left behind.'

The embers of the trampled fire were still glowing. Morgan kicked soil over them while Shani uprighted a three-legged cast iron cooking pot lying on its side on the ground. 'I wonder what they were going to cook for supper?' she mused. 'They told us they didn't have any food.'

Jake went towards the spot near the edge of the camp where he'd first seen the men. There was something on the ground – a black heap that looked like a boulder. Going closer, Jake realized that it was a dead bush pig. Around one of its legs was a tight wire noose. So that's what the men had been up to! They must have been about to start skinning the snared animal when Morgan called out to them. And that's why they had left in such a hurry the first time – they were afraid they'd be in trouble for killing game in Musabi.

Jake glanced over his shoulder. 'They were going to have bush pig for dinner,' he called to Shani.

Morgan and Shani hurried over.

'I guess if you're starving and have no food, you

have to hunt,' Jake said, reasonably. All the same, he couldn't help feeling angry that they'd killed an animal in Musabi, where all hunting was banned.

Morgan loosened the snare and slipped it off the pig's leg. 'This doesn't surprise me,' he said. 'But I think there's more to it than just snaring a meal. They had a gun, remember.'

'They could have been hunting bushmeat,' suggested Shani.

Morgan nodded. 'That's what I'm thinking.'

'But they can't do that here,' Jake protested angrily. Shani's words had reminded him of the grisly commercial trade in bushmeat that he'd witnessed in Uganda just weeks ago, where entire communities of chimpanzees were massacred for their meat.

Jake looked around the campsite, wondering how many other animals the men had killed during their short stay at the reserve. His eyes fell on a wide crack in the rock face. Something about it, a yellowy-white pointy object jutting out, made him look twice. 'What's that?' he muttered, going over to investigate.

Three steps away, Jake went cold. The pointed object was a tusk. And underneath it, better hidden in the gap, were several others.

'Morgan!' Jake yelled as he pulled out one of the tusks. It was about a metre long and must have weighed nearly twenty kilograms. 'Come and see this!'

'Sheesh!' breathed Morgan, coming over to Jake. His eyes were huge with concern. 'Those men are ivory poachers.'

Shani was staring at the tusk in disbelief. 'But they were such nice—' she began, then stopped abruptly. She turned her stricken gaze on Jake. '*That's* why they were so excited about Mlima,' she murmured.

'And why they were so keen to stay inside the reserve,' Jake added.

Just then, Rick's voice rang out through the bush. 'Morgan? Where are you? What's going on?' Jake guessed his stepdad had come to see how the fence was coming along and had heard the gunshot.

'We're here. At the cliff,' Morgan called back.

Rick appeared within a few seconds, followed by the farmers who'd stayed behind in the Land Rover.

'Who fired—' Rick began. Then he stared at the tusk cradled across Jake's arms. 'What the . . .?'

'We've just disturbed some poachers,' Jake told him.

'Poachers! In our reserve,' gasped one of the farmers. 'That is very bad.'

'Goliath gave them the fright of their lives,' added Shani.

Morgan quickly filled Rick in on the details. Rick looked stunned. 'We must get back to the house fast so that we can notify the police anti-poaching unit,' he said.

'Why don't you use the mobile phone?' suggested Shani, taking it out of her pocket.

'Good thinking,' Rick said. 'Let's hope we can pick up a signal out here.'

To everyone's relief, the phone was in range of a mast. Within a minute, the anti-poaching unit knew about the poachers. 'They'll be sending out trackers right away,' Rick announced after he'd finished describing the location.

'We will help to hunt them, too,' said one of the farmers earnestly. He clicked his tongue against the roof of his mouth and declared indignantly, 'How dare they come here and try to kill our elephants?'

Jake exchanged a surprised glance with Shani. Not two hours ago, the same man had been complaining about the elephants, saying they would trample his crops. But now he referred to them as 'ours'. Jake wondered if the threat from poachers had made him realize just how much the community stood to lose if any of the elephants were harmed.

'Finding the cell phone was a stroke of luck,'

remarked Rick, helping Morgan to pull out the rest of the tusks from the crevice. 'If you hadn't found their camp, who knows how much harm these men would have done before we realized what they were up to.' He heaved an enormous tusk on to one of his shoulders. 'We'll have to take these back to the house so the police can see them.'

In all, there were five pairs of tusks. They looked like smooth bleached tree branches. Jake felt a pang of sadness as he realized that somewhere in the bush – hopefully not in Musabi – lay the rotting carcasses of five elephants. Perhaps some of them had been females with calves – calves that were now orphans in need of rescuing, like Goliath. 'Why do you think Goliath charged them?' he asked Rick as they made their way back to the work site. Jake, like Shani, was carrying one of the smaller tusks.

Rick paused to shift the tusk on his shoulder so that it was more evenly balanced. 'I guess they must have surprised him, so he reacted instinctively and drove them off with a mock charge.'

'That was no mock charge,' said Morgan soberly. 'He meant every bit of it.'

Rick raised his eyebrows. 'Odd,' he commented, 'when you think how comfortable he is around humans.'

'Maybe not *all* humans,' suggested Shani. 'He might recognize poachers.'

Jake frowned at her. 'That's a bit far-fetched. *We didn't even know they were poachers at first, so how would Goliath be able to tell?'*

'Easy,' smiled Shani. She lifted the half metre long tusk she was carrying until it rested on her shoulders like a yoke. 'Because he's an elephant, and we're not. Perhaps that's why Goliath was orphaned all those years ago. Poachers might have killed his mother. And we all know that—'

'Elephants never forget,' Jake said, finishing Shani's sentence. *Could Goliath really have been seeking revenge for the killing of his mother?* he wondered. Jake felt a renewed wave of sympathy for the troubled lone elephant. Apart from feeling isolated in a strange territory, he might even be haunted by his last images of his mother, too.

News of the poachers' threat to the elephants seemed to spur the villagers on for the rest of that week. The fence was completed in record time, even without the help of the four strangers, who had disappeared without trace. The police had issued a warrant for their arrest, and a team of game rangers was scouring the surrounding areas, looking for the men.

On the day before Rosa's herd was due to be brought to Musabi, Rick arrived at the site to give the fence a final check. 'Excellent work,' he declared. 'Not even the strongest elephant will be able to get through this.'

Standing next to the fence with Shani, Jake listened to the regular pulsating click of the electric current as it passed through the wire. 'Are you sure?' he asked Rick. He glanced at the lush crops of maize, cabbages and bananas growing not far away on the other side of the fence. Jake could just imagine how inviting they would look to a hungry elephant. The ragged scarecrows the farmers had made to chase away birds would certainly not have much effect on an elephant!

'Pretty sure,' said Rick. 'Don't forget, Rosa's herd will be spending twenty-four hours in the boma before we let them out into the wider reserve, so they'll recognize an electric fence when they see one.'

The boma was a two acre electrified enclosure near to the Berman's house. The elephants would be released there when they came to Musabi. This would give them time to get over their long journey from Lufubu, and also to learn what an electric fence looked like.

'Right. Let's get going,' said Rick, striding back to

the Land Rover. He opened the door then looked back over his shoulder. 'Thanks again, everybody, for all your hard work,' he called to the villagers. Then, swinging himself into the driver's seat, he said, 'Come on, you two. I want to be in Rungwa before nightfall.'

Jake squashed up on the front seat next to Shani. All the doubts about the arrival of the new elephants disappeared as he started to focus on the critical schedule ahead of them. They were going to spend the night at the sanctuary then set out first thing in the morning for Lufubu in a helicopter that Don had borrowed from another sanctuary.

Jake had never been in a helicopter before. He could hardly believe that the very first time he went in one would be on an elephant capture operation! His new life in Africa was full of surprises.

EIGHT

The helicopter engine whined up to full power. Louder and faster it went, matching Jake's heart rate. Above, the rotor blades chopped round and round, creating a massive draft that whipped up a dust storm outside. Sitting in one of the small back seats next to Shani, Jake peered through his side window. The swirling dust had all but blocked out Rungwa's buildings. He could just make out Don's wife, Anita, waving from the veranda of the house in the morning sun.

'This is brilliant,' yelled Shani, her eyes sparkling with excitement. Like Jake, she'd never been in a helicopter before. But, unlike him, this was the first time she'd been in any type of aircraft. Still, excited as she was, she pulled a face and blocked her ears against the howling scream of the engine.

Don McClaren had taken the pilot's seat. Rick sat

next to him in the co-pilot's place, a gun resting on his lap. It was shaped like a rifle, but instead of bullets, it was loaded with tranquillizing darts that Rick would shoot at the elephants from the air.

Back at Musabi, when Jake was helping Rick to pack the darts into a special box, Rick had told him that they were filled with an immobilizing drug called M. 99 that would make the elephants slump quickly to the ground once they'd been shot. The darts also contained a sedative that would help to keep the elephants calm while they were being loaded into the transport lorries.

Rick adjusted the set of headphones he was wearing. Don had on a similar pair. The headphones had microphones attached to them so that the men could talk to one another above the whine of the helicopter, as well as to Mark once they were inside Lufubu.

With a final wave to Anita, Don pulled on the control stick. The four-seater helicopter lifted off the ground, causing an even bigger dust cloud that blocked Jake's view completely. But only for a moment, for the chopper was soon clear of the ground, and when Jake looked down out of his window again, he could see Anita still waving on the veranda and even some of the animals in their enclosures.

'Next stop, Lufubu,' said Don, shouting to make himself heard above the noise of the engine and the rotors. He pulled another lever. The helicopter pitched forward sharply, then started to fly steadily south, towards the Zambian border. Gazing out of his window at the bush sliding past beneath him, Jake glimpsed a herd of giraffes, galloping swiftly away from the noisy metal bird.

'Got the GPS, Jake?' Rick said loudly, turning round.

'Yes. In my backpack,' Jake answered.

'What's a GPS?' frowned Shani.

'A Global Positioning System. It tells you exactly where you are,' Jake told her.

'You mean, longitude and latitude and all that?' Shani asked.

'That sort of thing,' Jake nodded. 'Mark asked Rick if we had one. It'll help when we're locating the elephants.'

It only took half an hour to reach Lufubu where Mark was waiting with his team and a number of vehicles, including two big transport trucks. The vet was going to handle the ground operation once Rick had darted the elephants from the air.

Don put the helicopter down on a specially prepared landing field next to the game park's administration offices. With the rotor blades still spinning, Rick opened the curved glass door. 'Keep your heads down,' he warned Jake and Shani as they jumped out behind him.

Ducking until they were clear of the long blades, they ran across the field to Mark and his five helpers. Jake recognized some of them from the team who had been repairing the Lufubu fence the other day.

'All set to go?' Rick asked the vet.

'Yes. Although the elephants aren't making it easy for us,' replied Mark. 'Rosa's herd has teamed up with another one and we haven't seen them for a couple of days. But you should be able to spot them from the air.'

'You don't think they've broken out again?' Jake asked.

'No, we've checked the fence. It's intact all the way round,' answered Mark.

'Any idea what area of the park they're in?' Don asked the vet.

'I'd guess they're near that artificial water hole we recently dug in the north-east,' said Mark, spreading out a worn-looking map on the bonnet of his Land Rover and showing them the area he meant. 'We saw a lot of elephant prints in the mud there the other day.'

'Right. We'll head in that direction and keep you informed by radio,' Don told him, giving Mark the radio receiver he'd brought along. Then, turning to Jake and Shani, he said, 'Ready to do some aerial elephant hunting?'

'For sure!' Jake grinned, his excitement at fever pitch.

Rick cast him a doubtful glance. 'It's not going to be a tame helicopter flip,' he warned him. 'Don will probably have to separate the two herds. That's going to involve a lot of hovering and pitching. It'll definitely unsettle your stomachs, and it might even be dangerous. Perhaps you and Shani should stay on the ground.'

Stay on the ground? 'No way!' Jake insisted. 'Some rough flying doesn't scare me.'

'Nor me,' added Shani, although one look at her face told Jake she was definitely nervous.

'Herding elephants from the air isn't something you can do every day,' Jake added, to remind Shani as much as Rick.

'Well, don't say I didn't warn you,' said Rick with a mock sigh. 'Especially when you start feeling air sick.'

After they'd been flying for ten minutes, Don spotted the water hole. He swooped down and hovered above it, disturbing a herd of wildebeest that galloped away across the dusty plain.

'Nothing here,' Rick reported to Mark over the radio, and Don pulled on the control stick so that the helicopter pitched sharply to the right, then flew towards an area of thick bush that stood out in the barren landscape like a green oasis.

'Keep your eyes peeled,' Don shouted to Jake and Shani. 'If the elephants are down here, it'll be hard to see them.' He flew slowly over the dense vegetation, so low that Jake thought they might clip the tops of the trees.

'No sign of them,' said Don after a while. 'Let's go up higher for a wider view.'

'Wait!' Jake yelled. 'What's that?' He thought he'd seen something moving at the edge of a clearing. 'Near that baobab tree,' he added, and even as he said this, he saw the distinct bulky grey shape of an elephant making a frantic dash for cover.

At once, Don banked to the left and circled the clearing. Another elephant went charging into the bush, followed by several more.

'Well spotted, Jake,' shouted Don. Speaking into his microphone, he radioed the team on the ground. 'Elephants in sight.'

Rick checked the GPS and read out some numbers,

then Don described the exact location of the elephants. 'They're in thick bush at the moment,' he explained to Mark. 'But we should be able to drive them to a more suitable working area just north of here. See you shortly. Over and out.' He pushed the control stick up, and the helicopter pitched forward before flying slowly above the bush towards the hiding elephants.

Jake held his breath. He didn't like the idea of scaring the herd, but he understood that they had to move into a clearer space before Mark's ground crew could start work. Every now and then, he caught a glimpse of an elephant charging through the trees below. Eventually, the herd emerged on to the wide plain surrounding the water hole. Now that they were out in the open, Jake could see that the group of two families was about thirty strong.

One elephant stood out clearly from the rest. Rosa's gaunt, bony shape was unmistakable, even from the air. She was thundering along at the edge of the herd followed by the straight-tusked female that Jake recognized immediately as her sister.

'This is ideal,' said Don. 'Let's hope Rosa's group stays to one side like that.'

Jake couldn't help feeling sorry for the elephants. They looked utterly terrified, particularly the babies, who ran along blindly next to their mothers.

Shani also seemed troubled by their distress. Biting her fingernails, she stared wide-eyed out of her window.

Suddenly, Rosa veered away from the herd and ran towards the water hole. Nine others broke off to follow her while the rest of the elephants charged straight on.

'Excellent!' shouted Don. 'She's separated her group from the rest. Just what I hoped she'd do.' He pitched the helicopter to the right and flew above Rosa and her family.

Jake thought that the old matriarch looked even weaker than before. She ran past the drinking hole then, apparently exhausted, stopped some distance from it while the rest of the herd clustered around her, kicking at the ground and anxiously lifting their trunks.

'Poor old Rosa. She looks so wobbly!' shouted Shani. 'This is too much for her.'

'What if she has a heart attack?' Jake yelled, afraid that the stress of the chase was about to take its toll on Rosa.

'It's a chance we have to take,' said Rick calmly, slotting a dart into the chamber of the rifle. 'Hold her steady, Don.'

The pilot nodded then, to Jake's amazement, Rick slid open the helicopter door and leaned out, supported only by the straps on his seat harness.

Shani gasped. 'Careful!' she cried.

As steady as a rock, Rick took aim and tightened his finger around the trigger. But as he did so, Rosa looked up. She backed away, then, with her trunk raised in defiance at the whirring monster above her, she charged towards it. Even above the engine's din, Jake could hear her enraged scream, trumpeting out across Lufubu like an ancient war cry.

Galvanized by her courage, the rest of the herd surged forward beside her, forming a wall of grey that made it impossible for Rick to pick out any one individual.

'So much for your potential heart attack victim,' shouted Rick, lowering the dart gun.

'Yep! She's stronger than she looks,' said Don, making the helicopter rock left and right to break up the elephants. 'A threat from a big noisy bird won't finish her off.'

Far from scattering, Rosa's herd bunched together even more closely, with the smaller ones safely corralled in the middle. Jake shook his head in wonder. Hungry and hounded, the elephants had closed rank to protect the babies from harm.

'Drat!' shouted Rick. He called back over his shoulder to Don. 'We've got to break them up some more. If I dart any of them now, an adult could easily fall on a calf and flatten it. Also, I really need to get the matriarch first so that the herd doesn't scatter.'

'Righto,' said Don. 'I'll see what I can do.' He pulled the chopper out of the hover and pitched it forward to fly low over the herd. The elephants backed away, then turned and galloped off a short distance, taking refuge beneath the spreading branches of a solitary giant fig tree.

'We'll have to dart them from the ground if they stay there,' Rick shouted as he crouched in the doorway. 'I can't get a clear shot at them from up here.'

'OK. I'll find somewhere to land,' said Don. 'That flat bit near the water hole looks good enough.'

Rick sat back in his seat and held the dart gun upright on his lap. 'This is going to be dangerous,' he said over his shoulder to Jake and Shani as the chopper descended. 'I want the two of you to stay inside the helicopter once we've landed.'

Jake looked at Shani and pulled a face. The last thing he wanted to do was watch the capture from a safe distance. 'Oh come on, Rick,' he implored. 'We'll be careful. And we won't get in your way.'

'Maybe so. But there's no telling what the elephants will do. So I want you to stay here,' Rick repeated firmly.

Frustrated, Jake clicked his tongue against his teeth. 'We're not little kids,' he muttered under his breath.

'And you're not armed wildlife guards either,' Rick retorted, and Jake was surprised that his stepdad had heard his mumbled comment.

Jake sighed and stared out of his window, trying to hide his disappointment. *Overprotective adults*, he complained silently yet again. *They spoil all the fun.*

The helicopter landed with a cushioned bump about a hundred metres from the elephants, who looked out warily from their fig tree shelter. Rick unbuckled his harness and jumped out of the open door, the dart gun poised in his hands.

Jake folded his arms grumpily as Don turned off the engine.

'We'll let you know when you can get out,' Don said, unfastening his seat belt.

'Thanks,' Jake muttered unhappily. He looked out through the settling dust towards the water hole. A sudden movement in the churned-up mud at the water's edge caught his eye. 'What's that?' he said to Shani, sitting up straight.

'Where?'

'There. That grey blob in the mud.' Jake pointed, and then a terrible realization dawned on him as he recognized the shape of a head lying sideways, half hidden in the mud. 'It's an elephant!' he gasped. 'A calf, I think. It's stuck.'

'Oh yes. I can see it,' cried Shani, craning her neck to see past Jake. 'It's nearly buried!'

Forgetting Rick's stern instruction to stay where he was, and not even thinking of his own safety, Jake scrambled out of his seat. Someone had to rescue the little animal before it suffocated in the mud. He leaped to the ground, ducked beneath the still whirling blades and, almost knocking Rick over, charged past him towards the stricken calf.

'Hey! What do you think you're doing?' Rick yelled.

'There's a calf stuck in the mud,' Jake shouted back. 'We've got to rescue it before it drowns.'

'Wait!' Rick ordered.

But Jake kept going. He was sure there was no time to lose. Reaching the water hole in a matter of seconds, he saw that he was right. The calf was exhausted. It could barely keep its trunk from sinking below the mud. Any moment now, it wouldn't be able to breathe.

'Quick, come and help!' Jake shouted out, wading into the slimy mire. The thick brown mud seemed to want to suck him down into its swampy depths. He looked back to see if Rick was coming, but instead of his stepdad, a huge grey mass filled his view. In a split second, Jake recognized Rosa's sister. She was charging straight for him!

NINE

Thud! The elephant cow keeled over and landed heavily on her side just a few metres short of Jake. Jake felt his knees go weak as he realized what a narrow escape he'd had. One more big stride and the elephant would have crushed him. With his heart pounding wildly, he closed his eyes and took a deep breath.

He opened them again to see Rick running past the fallen elephant towards him, the darting rifle lodged in the crook of his elbow. One look at his stepdad was enough for Jake to know just how angry he was.

'That was the most stupid thing I've ever seen anyone do,' Rick snapped, reaching the edge of the drinking hole. 'And you made me take a real risk back there. You'd have been killed if the dart had missed the elephant and hit you instead.'

Jake looked down, feeling embarrassed. 'Sorry, Rick,' he muttered. 'It's just that . . .' He paused and glanced at the calf that was making another desperate attempt to escape its muddy prison.

'You can't save everything,' Rick told him, stretching out a hand to help Jake on to firm ground. 'Nature's bigger than you are.'

Jake gripped Rick's strong hand and stepped free of the oozing mud. He stamped his feet, trying to shake off some of the heavy clods which made his shoes feel as if they were made out of concrete. He felt the ground vibrate and, for a mad moment, was amazed that his feet could be *that* heavy until Rick said tensely, 'Now what?'

The answer came immediately in the form of the piercing scream of an enraged elephant – an elephant in full charge.

Even before he saw it, Jake knew who it was. 'Rosa!' he gasped hoarsely, the blood draining from his face as he recognized the trumpeting cry of defiance; the cry of a matriarch defending her threatened family.

Rick made a desperate attempt to reload his rifle. But it was too late. Rosa was already bearing down on them, her ears flapping and her trunk held high.

Jake thought he heard Rick shouting to him to run

but with several tons of elephant hurtling towards him, there was nowhere to go. Unless he tried to get back into the water hole. Finding the will to move, he spun round, and then froze as Rosa thundered straight past, ignoring him and Rick completely. She plunged into the mud, slowed down abruptly as it sucked at her legs, and fought her way out to the struggling calf.

With a gentleness that belied her enormous strength, the old matriarch pushed her tusks into the mud just behind the calf's back, while her trunk explored the infant's head.

His fear forgotten, Jake stood on the bank and watched, completely mesmerized. Now Rosa was using her tusks to lever the calf out of the mud. 'She's rescuing the baby,' Jake said quietly to Rick.

'She'll do her best,' said Rick, managing at last to reload his rifle. 'But she might not succeed. That calf looks pretty weak, I'm afraid. I think we'd better get out of the way while we can. Who knows what Rosa will do if she fails.'

They backed away slowly. When they were well clear of the water hole, they stopped again to watch. Don came over to join them, leaving a nervous-looking Shani peering out of the open door of the helicopter. 'I've radioed base to let them know we've started to dart the herd,' he told Rick. Like Jake's stepdad, he was carrying a loaded dart gun. 'We ought to keep an eye on the rest of the herd,' he warned. 'They're looking pretty restless.'

Over at the fig tree, the rest of Rosa's family shifted about nervously. They stamped the dusty ground and waved their trunks in the air, trumpeting from time to time as if discussing the next course of action.

'What happens now?' Jake asked Rick.

'We wait to see what Rosa does,' answered his stepdad. 'And hope the rest of the herd doesn't scatter in the meantime.'

The matriarch's tusks were now almost completely submerged in the mud. Patiently she worked away, elevating the calf bit by bit like an animated giant fork-lift truck picking up a heavy but fragile parcel. Before long, the calf was standing shakily upright, with only its feet under the mud.

'It's got to be able to get out of there now,' Jake muttered.

Rosa, however, seemed to think otherwise. She moved on to solid ground then stretched out her trunk and curled it gently round the calf's trunk. To Jake, it looked like she was offering the calf a helping 'hand' – in the same way that Rick had done to Jake just minutes before!

The calf lifted one front leg and took a hesitant step forward. Rosa tugged its trunk and the calf took another step. Several more tugs and steps later, the mud-encrusted little elephant was back on dry land, trotting over to its mother as if its brush with death had already been forgotten.

Rick and Don swung into action. With the calf a safe distance from Rosa, Rick took careful aim and shot a dart into the old female's shoulder. Looking utterly shocked, she turned round to see what had hit her. She managed to stagger forward a few more metres before the drug took effect and she collapsed on to the ground.

Don quickly darted the calf before it started to panic, then he and Rick moved across to the increasingly restless herd.

'Get back in the helicopter until the elephants are all down,' Rick called to Jake. 'And this time, I mean it!'

Jake really wanted to stay and watch Rick dart the others, but he knew better than to try his luck again. And two elephant charges were more than enough for one day! Still, he couldn't help thinking that a helicopter offered little protection against a charging elephant.

'Your guardian angels were looking after you

today,' said Shani when Jake climbed in next to her. Her eyes were still as wide as saucers. 'I thought we were going to have to scrape you out of the mud and take you home in an envelope.'

Jake shrugged, trying to appear nonchalant. 'I wasn't really in danger. Not with Rick nearby.'

'Oh, come off it, Jake,' retorted Shani. 'You were scared stiff!'

'Well, you try facing a charging elephant and see how you feel,' grinned Jake.

'I'll leave that to you,' Shani answered dryly. 'You're well experienced now.'

When Rick and Don were close enough, they began to dart the rest of Rosa's herd, expertly firing and reloading the rifles with smooth, deft movements. One by one, the elephants folded on to the ground until soon several huge grey bodies and a few smaller ones littered the landscape. One young bull had gone down on his chest with his legs tucked awkwardly beneath him, and Rick and Don started trying to push him over on his side.

'Let's help,' Jake suggested. He was sure it was OK to leave the helicopter now that all the elephants were down. He leaped out and ran over to the men, with Shani following close behind him.

They stood next to Rick and Don on one side of

the elephant and shoved with all their strength. But the heavy animal didn't budge. Jake felt as if they were trying to shift a solid lump of granite, albeit a warm, bristly one, with their bare hands.

'Why can't he stay on his chest like this?' he panted, turning round and digging his heels into the ground then pushing his back against the elephant.

'Because the weight of his stomach contents on his diaphragm will stop him from breathing,' Rick told him.

'Oh, right,' Jake said, shoving even harder.

They were still battling to roll the elephant on to his side when the ground crew arrived. First came Mark's Land Rover, then a truck that looked a bit like a mobile crane. Behind it came the two open-topped transport lorries, followed finally by another big truck towing a huge, flat-bed trailer.

The vehicles pulled up near the helicopter, and Mark and his team leaped out of the Land Rover and came running over to help with the bull. Working quickly, they tied ropes around the elephant's neck and middle, then everyone pulled on them until the bull finally flopped over on to his side, his top eye staring unblinkingly into the sky.

'A bit like having a tug-of-war with a giant,' Shani remarked to Jake. 'My arms are aching!'

'Mine too,' Jake agreed.

Mark was checking the elephant's heart rate and respiration with his stethoscope. 'Could one of you hold his trunk up for me, please?' he asked Jake and Shani. 'That'll help him breathe more easily. And the other can fold his ear over his eye to prevent it drying out.' He added, 'He can't blink while he's immobilized.'

While Shani gently positioned the huge ear flap, Jake lifted the trunk into the air. It was heavier than he had imagined, like an unwieldy sack of sand. 'How long do I have to hold it up?' he asked.

'Just until we load him,' said Mark. 'And I reckon we might as well start with him.' He beckoned to his team then said to Rick and Don, 'Would you supervise things this end while I monitor the breathing and heart rates of the other elephants?'

'Sure,' said Rick.

Straining to keep the limp trunk from slipping out of his hands, Jake watched the ground team prepare for the loading. First, the crane truck hoisted two big wooden crates off the truck that had arrived last and set them down at the back of the transport lorries.

'What are those boxes for?' Jake asked Rick who was helping Don untie the ropes around the bull.

'They're recovery boxes,' Rick explained. 'We put

the elephants in them until they come round, then we get them to walk up a ramp into the lorries.' He coiled up the rope and tossed it to one side.

'What's it like inside the lorries?' Jake wondered.

Don was pulling off the rope that was looped around the elephant's head. 'There are three compartments,' he explained. 'Depending on their size, two or three elephants will share each compartment. That way, they don't all fall on top of each other if the driver has to brake suddenly.'

'How do you get a sleeping elephant into the recovery box?' asked Shani, who was still crouching next to the bull's head, stroking the folded back ear.

'We hoist it on to the tip-up trailer and tow it across,' said Don. He started waving his arms, directing the crane truck in their direction. Next, the truck driver towed the trailer over, parking it a short way from the crane.

'OK. We're ready to move this one,' Rick said to Jake. 'You can let go of his trunk now.'

Jake gently lowered the trunk then stood to one side with Shani to watch. It would have been great to help to load the elephant, but he realized it was probably best to leave it to the experts and not get in the way.

Rick and Don pulled some heavy chains off the

trailer and fastened them around the elephant's legs while another man dragged a heavy piece of conveyor belting off the trailer and over to the sleeping elephant.

'Right. Lower the hook,' Don called to the crane operator.

The huge steel hook descended slowly until it was just above the elephant.

'Whoa!' shouted Don, grabbing the hook then hoisting one of the chains on to it. Rick did the same with another and soon all four chains that were tied around the bull's legs were attached to the crane.

'OK, lift,' ordered Rick.

Creaking loudly, the crane started to heave the heavy elephant off the ground. The motor droned, taking up the slack of the chains and gradually lifting the bull into the air.

'Just as well he's out cold,' remarked Shani. 'It must be horrible to be lifted up by your legs like that.'

'Especially if you weigh so much!' Jake agreed.

With the bull dangling feet upwards about a metre off the ground, the arm of the crane swung round then carefully lowered him on to the conveyor belting. The elephant rolled on to his side with a thud. Jake held his breath, wondering if all the movement and disturbance would wake the bull. But the elephant didn't stir.

Ducking out of the way of the crane, Rick unhooked the chains while Don and one of the Lufubu team tipped the back half of the trailer on to the ground, ready to receive its load.

'Give me a hand to secure him to the belting please, Jake,' called Rick, picking up one of the ropes lying on the ground.

Jake ran forward at once, thrilled to be involved again.

'Catch this,' said Rick. He threw the rope over the elephant's body. 'And loop it through the ring on the edge of the belting.'

Jake caught the end of the thick rope.

'Make sure you tie it tightly to the rings,' Rick warned. 'We don't want it coming loose and the elephant sliding off.'

'OK,' Jake said. He looped the rope through a ring and tied it into a reef knot, then did the same with two more ropes that Rick threw to him.

'Not bad,' said Rick approvingly, coming round to check that the elephant was well secured. 'Where did you learn to do reef knots so well?'

'On a sailing course when Mum and I were on holiday on the Isle of Wight,' Jake told him.

'Well, I couldn't have done better myself.' Rick smiled warmly and Jake felt a glow of pride.

Rick gave a thumbs-up signal to Don who was waiting at the back of the trailer. 'Right. Take him away,' he said.

Don reeled out a chain from a winch on the trailer and hooked it on to the conveyor belting. Whirring loudly, the battery-operated winch spooled the chain back in, dragging the elephant up the tipped-up trailer.

Rick and Don then righted the trailer so that the elephant was lying level once more.

'He looks like a very fat patient on a hospital trolley,' Shani chuckled.

Rick banged the side of the truck. 'OK. He's ready to roll,' he shouted, and the driver towed his heavy load across to one of the recovery boxes.

Jake and Shani jogged behind to watch the next stage of the elephant's long journey to his new home.

'It's going so smoothly,' Jake commented to Shani as the elephant was winched off the trailer and through the open doors of the recovery box. Inside, a ramp led up into the lorry.

'Let's hope it carries on like this,' said Mark who had followed them. He opened his vet's bag and took out a big syringe and a phial. He plunged the needle into the glass bottle and drew up the liquid inside.

'What's that for?' Shani asked the vet.

'It's the antidote,' said Mark, going into the box. 'To bring him round again.'

Jake and Shani stood to one side next to the open doors and watched the vet clamber over the elephant's outstretched legs. Reaching the animal's head, he injected the antidote into one of his ears.

Jake winced, but he guessed that elephants had pretty tough skin. 'How long will it take to work?' he asked Mark, who was backing rapidly out of the recovery box.

'About a minute,' said the vet, closing the doors and sliding a strong metal bar across them.

Peering through the slats, Jake anxiously watched the elephant. As Mark had promised, the medication started working very quickly. The elephant blinked and shook his head, then heaved himself over on to his front. Within about three minutes he was up on his feet, looking rather dazed but none the worse for his experience.

Jake half expected the young bull to start going crazy, trying to find a way out. But the tranquillizer must still have been working because he was surprisingly peaceful, and made no fuss about walking up the ramp into the back of the lorry.

'That looked easy,' Jake said, shaking his head in amazement. He could hear the floorboards of the lorry creaking under the weight of the bull, but that was the only noise the elephant made.

'They're not always that obliging,' said Mark, signalling to one of his men to close the lorry's doors. 'The tranquillizer can make them a bit too sleepy. Or sometimes they're just plain stubborn. So we have to prod some of them to make them walk into the lorry.'

It took about four hours for all the elephants to be loaded. In that time, Jake and Shani helped by gently pouring water on to the waiting elephants' ears to keep them from overheating. They also made sure that all their trunks were straight so that their airways weren't blocked, and Jake was kept busy tying his famous reef knots every time an elephant was hoisted on to the conveyor belting.

Finally, with the sun beating down mercilessly, there was only one more elephant to load. The matriarch, Rosa.

Lying still and bound by ropes on the conveyor belting, she looked to Jake more like the pathetic victim of a hunting expedition than the brave matriarch that had charged at the helicopter to protect her herd. Loose grey skin sagged round her face, and her backbone stood out sharply like the edge of a rocky ridge. Still deeply sedated, she stared vacantly with sad brown eyes that were deeply sunken into her head.

Once inside the recovery box, and with the antidote taking effect, Rosa struggled to get up. Breathing heavily, she stamped one foot on the ground then uttered a deep rumble. In reply, a low rumbling chorus came from inside the three lorries.

'At least she knows the rest of her family is close by,' said Shani.

'I bet she's confused though,' Jake said, peering through a big gap in the wooden slats.

Rosa dabbed at the air with her trunk as if she was trying to work out where she was. She turned her head, and for a moment her gaze met Jake's. Now that she was fully conscious, there was no longer a vacant expression in her eyes, but a look of deep anxiety.

'It's OK,' Jake murmured. He felt a wave of sympathy for the old animal, even regret at having to move her from the home range where she and her family had trodden the same paths as all their ancestors had done. But then, the alternative was a lot worse.

Don gently prodded Rosa to send her into the lorry. She took a step forward, then turned her head and locked eyes with Jake again, uttering another low, throaty grumble.

'Don't worry,' Jake told her. He managed to slide one hand through the wooden slats so that the tips of his fingers just brushed against her tough leathery hide. 'You're going to a place where there's plenty to eat and where you can live in peace with your family. No one's going to threaten you in Musabi,' he promised.

Rosa blinked at him, then turned and padded slowly up the ramp, until the doors slid shut behind her.

TEN

The transport lorries and their bulky cargo arrived at Musabi in the small hours of the next morning. Jake had slept off and on throughout the long journey, squashed up next to Shani on the front seat of the lorry that Rick was driving, but he woke up when they rumbled over the cattle grid at the entrance to the reserve.

'Musabi at last,' he said, rubbing his eyes and looking out at the dark bush all around them. He took a swig from one of the bottles of water they'd bought in a town some time during the night. He felt a mounting excitement. It was going to be brilliant to see the elephants released into the boma. But he also wondered how they would behave. 'Will there be a bit of a stampede when the doors are opened?' he asked Rick.

'There could be,' replied his stepdad, slowing

down as they turned a sharp bend. 'Mark will be giving all the adults another tranquillizer before we offload them. We don't want them to injure themselves after we've got them this far.' He yawned and shifted in his seat. 'I'm looking forward to getting out of this lorry myself. And to snatching a bit of sleep before the sun rises.' He glanced at the side mirror which reflected the lights of the second lorry not far behind them. 'Mark's probably thinking the same thing right now.'

Mark had driven the other lorry up from Zambia, while Don had flown the helicopter back to its owners. He would be coming to Musabi in a day or two to return Rick's Land Rover that was still parked at Rungwa.

Unlike Jake, Shani had slept soundly for most of the trip, curled up on the seat between Jake and Rick. She must have heard them talking, for she opened her eyes and looked up. 'Are we there yet?' she asked sleepily.

'Uh-huh. Just a few more kilometres before we get to the boma,' Rick told her.

Shani sat up and yawned, then clasped her hands behind her head and stretched. 'Anything left to drink?'

Jake passed her a bottle of water. 'I guess the

elephants could do with some too,' he said.

'Well, there's plenty of water for them in the troughs in the boma,' Rick commented. He turned the lorry on to the road that led to the enclosure that would be the elephants' home for the next two days. It was just below the Bermans' house. A fenced walkway between the garden and the boma provided a protected short cut so that Rick didn't have to drive all the way round whenever he needed to check on the animals being kept in the enclosure.

The lorry's headlamps cut through the inky darkness and lit up the tall fence just ahead. Jake leaned forward in his seat. The herd's ordeal was almost at an end. In just a few days, they'd be free to wander throughout Musabi, their safety assured at last. At least, he *hoped* they'd be perfectly safe. 'I wonder if the police have tracked down those ivory poachers yet?' he asked.

Rick grimaced. 'Not as far as I know – unless, of course, something happened while we were at Lufubu. Although I doubt that. Your mum would have let us know.' A few metres short of the boma, he turned the lorry and backed it up until it was just a short distance from the wide gate.

Jake flung open his door and jumped down to

the ground, glad to stretch his legs at last. Rick and Shani climbed out too, then they watched as Mark parked nearby, leaving the headlamps on to light up the area.

'That must be one of the longest nights ever,' the vet grunted, getting out of his cab and stretching. Another man climbed out of the lorry. He was Mark's assistant, Shadrack, who had travelled with him from Lufubu. The two men would be spending the next night at Musabi, then driving the two lorries back to Zambia the following day. 'OK, Shadrack. Let's get going with the tranquillizers,' said Mark, taking his vet's bag out of the cab.

The two Lufubu men climbed up the sides of the lorries and began skilfully injecting the tranquillizing drug into the adult elephants' ears.

'Just as well the lorries don't have roofs,' remarked Shani, watching the vet edging his way nimbly round the top of the vehicle. 'I wouldn't fancy having to get right inside to inject the elephants.'

An owl called out from a nearby tree-top. *Vooo-hu*, it hooted into the darkness. *Voo-wu-hu*, came the mellow reply of its mate. From inside the lorries came a few creaking noises and some low rumbling sounds, but apart from these and the owls' plaintive duet, there was silence.

'We'll give the drug about fifteen minutes to work, then we'll start offloading,' said Mark, jumping down from the second lorry.

'I could do with a cup of coffee in the meantime,' said Rick. 'Any chance of you and Shani organizing some for us?' he asked Jake.

'Sure. Just as long as you don't let the elephants out before we get back,' Jake teased. He took a torch from the cab of the lorry then he and Shani started up the walkway to the house.

Suddenly, Shani stopped and grabbed Jake's arm. 'What's that?

'What?' Jake asked, but before Shani could answer, Jake heard a familiar noise. Below the high-pitched chorus of a million crickets, there was a rumble of throaty bass notes. 'Elephant,' Jake whispered and he flashed his torch through the fence in the direction of the sound. The yellow beam lit up trees and ant-heaps, and even the bright eyes of a cat-like genet which quickly dived behind a rock. But there was no sign of an elephant.

'Must be one of Rosa's herd,' Jake decided. He shone the torch ahead and carried on along the walkway. 'Come on. Let's hurry. We've only got a few minutes.' He quickened his pace then stopped so abruptly that Shani bumped into him.

'Now what?' she said.

'I can see the elephant,' Jake whispered. 'Dead ahead, next to the fence. I bet it's Goliath.' He held the torch steady. The beam fell on a wrinkled face, the familiar right-angled tusk casting a sharp black shadow across his chest.

'It's Goliath all right,' breathed Shani.

'Hello, Big G,' Jake murmured.

Goliath stood completely still, staring straight ahead.

'What's up?' Jake continued. 'You're not begging for bananas in the middle of the night, are you?'

'Maybe he's heard the new elephants?' suggested Shani.

'If he had, he wouldn't be anywhere near here,' Jake pointed out. 'He'd probably be heading in the opposite direction, like he always does when he sees other elephants.'

With that, Goliath flapped his ears then turned and walked silently away.

'I think he heard you,' chuckled Shani.

'Funny elephant,' said Jake, struck more than ever by the contrast between the antisocial young bull and tightly knit family groups like Rosa's herd.

They were just entering the garden through the

latched wooden gate when the torchlight picked out a figure coming across the lawn towards them.

'It's Mum,' said Jake, waving.

Hannah was carrying a big wicker basket containing several flasks and mugs, as well as a tin of biscuits. Her camera was slung over one shoulder. 'Hi, you two,' she said. 'On your way to bed?'

'You must be joking!' Jake exclaimed. 'Rick wanted some coffee so we were coming to fetch it for him. It looks like you beat us to it.'

'Telepathy,' chuckled Hannah. 'Actually, I heard the lorries arriving and knew you'd all need something to keep you going for a while. Come on, you can give me a hand with this basket.'

Back at the boma, Hannah poured out mugs of steaming coffee for the adults, and hot chocolate for Jake and Shani. Then, at last, after their long journey from Zambia to Tanzania, it was time for the elephants to be offloaded. Rosa was going to be the first one out.

Rick reversed his lorry closer to the enclosure. He leaned out of his window and called to Jake, 'Let me know when the back's tight up against the gate.'

'Will do,' Jake said. He stood next to the fence and waved Rick on. Above the thrum of the engine, he could hear the steady *click-click* of the electric pulses flowing through the strands at the top of the fence. When there was just a small gap between the back of the truck and the boma, Jake whistled loudly.

Rick cut the engine and swung himself down from the cab, then he and Mark slid open the back door while Shadrack let down the ramp.

Jake felt a thrill of anticipation. Next to him, Hannah had her camera at the ready, and Shani was nervously biting a thumbnail. But apart from the strong gamey odour that floated out from the lorry, there was no sign of an elephant.

Mark banged on the side of the truck. 'Come on, Rosa,' he encouraged her. 'This is where you get off.' He banged again. A loud creak answered him from inside. Seconds later, Jake saw the tip of a trunk probing the air just outside the open door, then at last Rosa emerged from the dark interior and stood at the top of the ramp.

'Welcome to Musabi,' Jake whispered. He heard Hannah's camera click, accompanied by the dazzling flare of the flashbulb.

Rosa blinked, but the tranquillizer kept her calm. She shook her head so that her ears flapped loudly before taking a tentative step forward. Looking around cautiously, she waved her trunk from side to side then, as if she had made up her mind, she plodded down the ramp and into the boma.

Moments later, her sister emerged with her calf between her legs. They followed the matriarch into their temporary refuge while behind them came the two young bulls that made up the rest of the lorry's cargo.

As Rick quietly closed the gates, the elephants took a few steps forward, then stopped and stood together in a tight group, their faces lit up by the beam coming from the headlights of Mark's lorry.

'They look really confused,' Jake whispered to Shani.

The five elephants blinked and gazed around as if they were trying to make out where they were.

'I bet they know they're not at Lufubu,' said Shani. 'It's really different here with so many trees and bushes.'

Rick backed the empty truck away a short distance then turned it round, training the headlamps on the boma so that the whole process could be repeated with the rest of the herd in the second lorry.

The five remaining elephants moved easily into the enclosure until, finally, the lorry's headlights were switched off and all ten elephants huddled together, quietly testing the ground with the sensitive tips of their trunks. Standing almost completely still, they formed a bulky mound in the soft grey mist that accompanied the half light of dawn.

Jake stood with the others near the fence. He listened to the soft puffing of the elephants' breathing and the murmuring rumble of their conversation. 'I wonder what they're saying?' he said quietly.

'Probably just reassuring each other that all's well,' Hannah replied. 'If they were anxious, they'd be making a lot of other noises.'

Still surprised at how smoothly everything had gone, Jake murmured, 'I never thought they'd be this peaceful.'

'Well, they are sort of half asleep,' Shani reminded him.

'So am I,' said Rick. He slapped a mosquito that had settled on his arm. 'Come on, everyone. Let's get to bed. We can check on these guys when the sun comes up.'

Half an hour later, Jake lay in bed, staring up at the ceiling and thinking about everything that had happened in the last twenty-four hours: the helicopter flight; the herding of the elephants from the air; the two terrifying charges; the darting of the big animals. But what kept coming back to him most of all was the way Rosa had defended her family and kept them together, right to the point of pulling a calf out of the mud in the midst of a bunch of humans who had terrorized her from the air. *That was so awesome*, Jake thought.

Since coming to live in Musabi, he'd learned how close elephant families were, but he'd never realized just how loyal they could be. *And intelligent*, he remembered, picturing again the way Rosa had used her tusks and trunk to free the calf.

He turned over and shut his eyes and felt himself drifting off to sleep. Somewhere in the reserve, a lion roared and a bushbaby shrieked. The rumbling roar and piercing shriek came again. Instantly, Jake was fully awake. *Lion? Bushbaby? No way! More like elephants*.

He sprang out of bed and flung open his windows. The sun was just peeping above the horizon, turning the bush red and gold. Jake held his breath and listened to the strange noises. They seemed oddly intense, almost desperate even. And what was more, they were coming from the direction of the boma.

'It's definitely the elephants,' Jake decided. 'Something's going on!' Not even stopping to pull on his shoes, he tore outside to investigate.

Barefoot, he raced down the walkway, his heart in his mouth. Another desperate trumpeting cry echoed in the misty morning air. An elephant in trouble? Or in pain? 'Please don't let it be the poachers!' Jake prayed aloud.

He thrust open the gate at the end of the walkway and dashed past the two parked lorries to the enclosure. He had no idea what he would do if the four men from the north *were* there. All he knew was that the elephants could be in grave danger.

And just when they should have been safe! he thought angrily. Then he stopped short, stunned by the scene that greeted him. Standing just metres away, right next to the boma fence, was Goliath. Facing him on the other side was Rosa. And high above the electric wire, their trunks were intertwined like two thick snakes curling around each other.

'Goliath!' Jake gasped. He blinked. Was he dreaming this? But no, the elephants were real.

He stared at the pair in wonder. Every now and then, one of them would utter an excited trumpeting cry, or make a throaty rumble which travelled through the ground and vibrated under Jake's bare feet. Jake was flummoxed. Of all the elephants in Musabi, Goliath had to be the least likely to welcome the new group. If, in fact, that was what he was doing.

Meanwhile, the rest of Rosa's herd bumped and jostled behind her, like people growing restless in a queue. Some of them stamped the ground and shook their trunks, or trumpeted with excitement.

Jake realized that the tranquillizers were wearing off. He hoped that chaos wasn't about to break out. Perhaps he'd better call Rick. He turned to go, but the creak of the gate at the end of the walkway made him pause. He looked across and saw Morgan coming towards the boma. Morgan had been staying in the guest cottage next to the Bermans' house. He must have heard the disturbance too.

Jake ran to meet him. 'You'll never believe what's happened,' he told Shani's uncle.

Together they stood and watched Rosa and Goliath. Their urgent rumbles and shouts grew more frequent, while the rest of the herd was also growing more animated.

'It's like Goliath's come to welcome them,' said Jake.

Morgan folded his arms and shook his head slowly. 'There's more to it than that,' he said.

'Like what?' Jake asked, puzzled.

'Rosa and Goliath *are* greeting each other,' said Morgan. 'But not as strangers. More like friends.'

Jake was taken aback. 'Friends!' he echoed. 'That's impossible.'

Morgan shrugged. 'Apparently. But I'm telling you for sure that those two elephants know each other. Where they've met, I don't know. But what I do know is that they've met before today.'

ELEVEN

'No way! That's crazy!' Jake shook his head. Goliath had always gone out of his way to avoid other elephants for as long as he'd been at Musabi. Jake frowned at Morgan as a more logical idea struck him. 'You don't think Goliath wants to side with Rosa's herd because they're strangers here, like he was two years ago?'

'I don't think so. If anything, he'd be very wary of a new group,' Morgan replied.

Jake still couldn't accept Morgan's explanation. 'But how *can* they have met? Goliath was in Rungwa for ten years before he came here. And Lufubu's a long way from Rungwa, even for an elephant.' Surely Rosa couldn't have trekked all the way across the border to the sanctuary during one of her breakouts from Lufubu.

Morgan nodded. 'We'll probably never know the

full story. But one thing's for sure. Goliath's not the loner we all thought he was.'

'It looks like it,' Jake agreed. He suddenly realized that even though Goliath must have known he and Morgan were there, for once he wasn't interested in the humans. He was completely focussed on Rosa.

But he was also growing frustrated. Grumbling loudly, he disentangled his trunk from Rosa's and stamped the ground, then started pacing restlessly back and forth along the fence. Inside the boma, Rosa kept pace with him.

'I hope those two don't try to push the fence down,' Jake said.

'They've probably already tried,' said Morgan. 'So they'll know all about electricity now.'

'Ouch!' Jake sympathized, imagining what it must be like to lean against a wire fence and, quite literally, get the shock of your life.

The elephants' cries soon brought Rick and Hannah to the boma too. Like Jake, Rick's first thought had been that the herd was in trouble, so he'd come armed with his rifle. And when he saw what was really going on, he was just as flabbergasted as Jake.

'It just doesn't add up,' he said, while Hannah, who was almost never without her camera, took photographs of the extraordinary scene. 'Anyone would think those two knew each other.'

'That's what Morgan thinks, too,' Jake told him, exchanging a glance with Shani's uncle. He looked back towards the house, wondering if Shani had heard the commotion yet. But there was no sign of her. Jake guessed she must still be dead to the world after their long night.

The sun had climbed above the horizon. The first bright rays reached across Musabi like giant yellow tentacles, sucking up the early morning mist and covering the land in a clear golden glow; a promise of the heat yet to come. And all around, rush hour in the bush was in full swing.

Birds dived and swooped, plucking insects out of the air, while others breakfasted on seeds and berries or scratched in the ground to uncover juicy worms. Further afield, zebras greeted the dawn with their characteristic bark, and guinea fowls shattered the peace with their raucous, metallic chattering. Somewhere from his tree-top roost, a baboon shrieked out an alarm call that was met by similar cries from others in the troop. And amid all the bushveld buzz, Goliath and Rosa relentlessly paced the fence.

Minutes behind Rick and Hannah, Mark and

Shadrack arrived at the boma, followed, at last, by a bleary-eyed Shani. Tripping along behind her came Bina, the orphaned dik-dik.

'Is that Goliath?' Shani burst out disbelievingly when she saw the elephant reaching towards Rosa again with his trunk.

'That's him all right,' Morgan confirmed.

'Isn't it brilliant?' Jake said to Shani. 'Goliath isn't so antisocial after all.'

Goliath let out another shout of frustration and trotted a few metres towards his human audience, then stood and faced them.

Jake met the elephant's gaze full on. Goliath uttered a low rumble, almost as if he was trying to communicate with Jake. 'Do you think he's asking us to let Rosa come out?' Jake wondered out loud.

'What's so special about Rosa?' Shani frowned, scooping up Bina who had been heading for the electric fence. 'I mean, apart from being a wise old matriarch?'

'I don't know,' Jake admitted. 'But there's definitely something going on between them.'

'Hang on a sec.' Mark was staring at Goliath. 'Well, I never,' he said slowly, shaking his head.

'What is it?' Jake asked, seeing a look of amazement on the vet's face.

'That young bull. I know him,' said Mark.

'Well, he comes from Rungwa,' Hannah pointed out. 'That's probably where you saw him.'

'But I've never been to Rungwa,' Mark told her. 'And the last time I saw this elephant – Goliath, as you call him – was when he was just a few months old. And that was in Zambia.'

'Zambia!' Jake exclaimed. 'That's impossible!'

Rick looked equally surprised. 'Goliath's nearly twelve now,' he told Mark. 'How can you be sure he's the same elephant you're talking about?'

'That tusk.' Mark pointed to Goliath's right-angled tusk. 'It was exactly like that when he was an infant, only shorter and thinner, of course.' He looked at Shani. 'You put your finger on the answer,' he said to her.

Shani looked at him with big eyes. 'I did?'

'Uh-huh. You said Rosa was a wise old matriarch,' the vet continued. 'And that's exactly what makes her so special to Goliath. And it's the only explanation that makes any sense.' He paused while Rosa and Goliath once more locked trunks above the fence.

Jake waited for Mark to go on but his impatience quickly got the better of him. 'Well, it still doesn't make sense to me,' he said. 'I mean, Rosa's not the only matriarch in Musabi.'

'As far as Goliath's concerned, she is,' said Mark. His blue eyes shone as he grinned at Jake. 'You see, she's the matriarch of the herd he belonged to. Rosa is Goliath's great-aunt.'

Goliath's great-aunt! Jake repeated in his head. 'So his mother was Rosa's niece?' he said slowly to Mark, trying to get a handle on it all.

'That's right,' Mark confirmed. 'The herd used to be a lot bigger, but I knew most of the individuals pretty well. I had to monitor their behaviour as part of a study on elephant migration I was doing at the time. Their home range extended beyond Lufubu's borders and even across the Zambian border. In those days, the human population was a lot smaller so the elephants hardly ever came into close contact with people. At least, not until poachers arrived in the area.'

'And they killed Goliath's mother?' Jake said.

Mark looked grim. 'Uh-huh. And many of the other adults. Within a few months, the herd was halved. That's when we started fencing them in to protect them.' He stared at Goliath. 'When this young fellow and his mother went missing, I was almost sure he'd been killed alongside her.'

'But instead, someone found him wandering alone in the bush,' Rick finished off the story. 'And that's when he was taken to Rungwa. No one knew where his family was and Don and Anita assumed that they must have all been killed.'

'Now they've all ended up at Musabi,' breathed Shani, her voice filled with wonder.

'It really is the most incredible coincidence,' said Hannah, snapping more pictures of Goliath and his long-lost family. 'And to think that after more than eleven years, the two should remember each other.'

Jake exchanged a grin with Shani. 'That's not hard to understand really,' he said. 'As Shani's always saying . . .'

'Elephants never forget,' chuckled Shani.

Goliath kept close to the boma for the rest of the day. Jake and Shani returned several times to watch the elephants, and even though both Rosa and Goliath seemed to accept that the fence was keeping them apart, neither of them moved far from the electric barrier. Jake was convinced that now the lonely bull had found his family, he was determined not to leave them again. He was really impressed by Goliath's loyalty to his original herd, which had kept him from joining up with an unrelated group in the two years he'd been at Musabi.

'I can't wait to see what he'll do when we let the herd out of the boma,' Jake said to Shani when they were returning to the house for supper. The elephants seemed to have adapted well so Rick planned to release them early the next morning.

'He'll probably just go trotting off into the bush with them,' said Shani in her usual down-to-earth way.

'I guess so,' Jake said. 'After all, they've already said hello about a hundred times today. They must be dying to get on with all the normal herd stuff!'

'Perfect,' said Rick when the Bermans and Shani arrived at the boma at first light the next day. Mark and Shadrack had left before dawn, hoping to make Lufubu before nightfall, while Morgan had gone to Sibiti to inform Julius that the elephants were about to be released into the wider reserve.

'The herd's nowhere near the gate, so we can open it without being stampeded!' Rick said with a grin.

'I'll help you,' Jake offered. He could see Goliath browsing on a Mopane tree close to where Rosa and the others were feasting on some low bushes near the far end of the boma.

Jake and Rick unlocked the gate – the only part of the fence that wasn't electrified – and swung it open.

'I just hope they realize they can get out now,' Jake said as he and Rick joined the others who were watching from behind the screen gate at the end of the walkway.

'They'll find out soon enough,' Rick promised.

But it was Goliath who saw the opening first. Still clutching a branch in his trunk, he ambled over and stopped just short of the gate. He stuffed the branch into his mouth then, munching the leaves, looked cautiously around.

'Come on, Goliath,' murmured Shani. 'You can always have breakfast later. Go and meet your great-aunt.'

Goliath stared into the boma. Then he lifted his trunk and trumpeted loudly, as if calling out to Rosa.

The matriarch looked up. Goliath trumpeted again. Rosa held her huge ears at right angles to her head, listening to the call, then she turned slowly and padded towards Goliath. Behind her came the rest of the herd in single file, like an orderly procession of giants. It was a far cry from their frenzied behaviour when Rosa had tried to lead them away from the helicopter. Now they followed her calmly through the gate as if they knew there was no danger here.

Goliath watched his family emerge from the enclosure. With what sounded to Jake like a shout of triumph, he lifted his head and let out a deafening cry. It echoed through the bush, silencing everything else. And then the two long-separated elephants came together in an embrace that left even Jake damp-eyed.

Standing wrinkled face to wrinkled face, Rosa and Goliath rubbed their foreheads together and tenderly patted each other with the tips of their trunks. The remaining nine elephants clustered around the pair, uttering low rumbles of pleasure.

Hannah's camera clicked constantly.

'I think the dung beetle article will have to be sidelined for now,' Rick said to his wife.

'Absolutely!' Hannah agreed enthusiastically. 'This story is unique.'

'Yeah, I can't imagine two dung beetles meeting up like this,' laughed Shani.

The tender reunion continued. At one point Rosa looked across, and her eyes briefly met Jake's. Gone was the look of misery she wore when Jake had first seen her. In its place was the air of serenity Jake had come to associate with the other herds of elephants in Musabi. Elephants who didn't have to fear for their safety, and who weren't hungry and thirsty, who had enough territory to roam in, without feeling caged-in.

But there was another dimension to Rosa's

expression. 'I wonder if finding Goliath has helped to make up for her daughter being shot?' Jake suggested.

'Could be,' said Rick. 'She certainly doesn't look depressed any more.'

'And Goliath looks like he's landed in paradise,' grinned Shani.

'Too right he does,' Jake chuckled as Goliath peered over Rosa's trunk towards him. It could have been his imagination, but Jake was sure that the young bull had actually winked.

Eventually Rosa drew back from Goliath and surveyed her new surroundings. All around, the land was covered in tall grass and dense green bushes, while just behind the boma, a healthy forest of Mopane trees beckoned invitingly. At the bottom of a steep slope at the edge of the trees, a wide river glinted in the morning sun.

The wise old elephant sniffed the air and walked around in wide circles while the others stood patiently waiting. Goliath seemed content to let Rosa decide where she would lead them first.

Finally, she made up her mind. Swishing her thin tail, she set off purposefully, passing just in front of Jake and the others, then making her way down the steep slope. The rest of the herd followed, with

Goliath immediately behind her.

'She's taking them to the river,' Jake said.

'It must be a wonderful sight for them,' Hannah pointed out, 'especially after they've been without a natural water supply for so long.'

Rick put an arm round Hannah's shoulders and hugged her. 'Well, that's that,' he said happily. 'A successful translocation.'

'It was more than that,' Hannah reminded him. 'It was also a family reunion.'

'Yes. I think we should let Don and Anita know about that,' said Rick. 'Let's give them a call.' Looping his arm through Hannah's, he started back for the homestead.

Jake and Shani stayed behind to watch the elephants go for their first swim in Musabi. They climbed up a nearby tree so that they could have a grandstand view.

Rosa was halfway down the slope to the river when she stopped abruptly and turned round. The herd stopped too.

'Now what?' said Jake.

Rosa was standing in front of Goliath, as if she was blocking his way. Goliath reached out with his trunk and touched her lightly on her face.

'More lovey-dovey stuff,' chuckled Shani.

'You'd think that was all over for now,' said Jake. But then, to his dismay, he saw that the display of affection *was* over as Rosa pushed Goliath away with her head before turning and continuing down the slope.

Confused, Goliath loped after her but Rosa stopped and shoved him away again, this time a lot more persistently. Goliath took a few steps back, while the rest of the herd pushed past him, their attention fixed on Rosa.

'What's going on?' Jake murmured.

Goliath stood for a moment, staring after his family then, with a shake of his head, set off after them again. But Rosa was having none of it. She whirled round and charged back up the slope to Goliath. Jake and Shani gasped as the matriarch butted the young elephant with her head so hard that he stumbled backwards. Her message was clear. Goliath was not to follow her.

'She's rejecting him,' Jake burst out, appalled.

'But he's her family,' protested Shani.

'It doesn't look like it any more,' Jake remarked tersely as Rosa spun round and trotted down the slope to the others. The grim reality of the situation hit Jake like a fence mallet. Goliath was destined to be a loner after all.

TWELVE

Driven out from the herd, Goliath stood on the hill and watched Rosa leading the others to the river. Jake could hardly believe how quickly Goliath's fortunes had changed – from bad to good then, almost without warning, back to bad. And one look at Goliath was enough to tell just how much he was feeling this latest blow. After his brief experience of being part of a caring family group once more, he looked utterly bereft.

'It probably would have been better if he hadn't recognized Rosa,' Jake said gloomily. 'At least that way he wouldn't have known what he was missing.'

'But he must have been missing his family all along,' Shani pointed out. 'That's why he changed so much when he saw Rosa.' She waved away a fly that was buzzing round her face. 'I wonder why Rosa doesn't want him in the herd? I mean, there's plenty for them to eat here.'

Jake shook his head. 'It's really odd, especially as Rosa cheered up too when she saw Goliath.' He sighed. 'Poor old fellow. I bet he's more puzzled than we are.'

But Goliath hadn't given up yet. Seeing Rosa and the others go splashing into the river must have been more than he could bear, for he went charging after them, trumpeting as if to say, *'Wait for me. I'm coming too.'*

Rosa was standing in the shallows of the river with her trunk looped into her mouth. When she heard Goliath's call, she stopped drinking and calmly watched her long-lost nephew running towards the herd.

Jake's hopes rose. 'It looks like Rosa's changed her mind,' he said.

But the instant Goliath set foot in the water, Rosa rushed at the young bull, driving him back on to dry land. She skidded to a stop on the muddy shore and glared at him, flapping her ears menacingly.

Looking thoroughly dejected, Goliath retreated up the bank. At the top, he stared down at the herd in the river. The tiny calves were having a great time. They rolled and splashed in the water, churning up the bottom so that the river quickly became a cauldron of swirling mud. Several of the adults moved patiently away to where the river was undisturbed. Standing together in a straight row, almost as if they were posing for a photograph, they siphoned up the clean, cool water.

Rosa strolled over to the row of adults. But instead of dipping her trunk into the river, she edged her way in between two individuals and gently bumped against them.

'What's she doing now?' Jake frowned, leaning forward on the branch he was sitting on so that he could get a better look.

'Pushing in, so she gets the best spot?' suggested Shani.

Rosa kept nudging the two elephants until they backed out of the water.

'She really is the boss. No one argues with her,' Jake commented, and with a regretful glance at Goliath he added, 'It's almost a pity she does have so much power. Goliath might be standing in the river right now if she wasn't so bossy!'

The two elephants walked away from the river. Jake expected them to join another member of the herd that was feasting at a fig tree laden with fruit, but they kept going, heading back the way they'd come – up the slope towards Goliath who stood stock still watching them.

Jake recognized one of them by a distinctive tear in his right ear. 'That's the bull that went down on his chest when Rick darted him,' he reminded Shani. The young elephant was about the same size as Goliath and his tusks were as straight and sharp as swords.

A welcome thought struck Jake. 'Maybe Rosa has sent them to bring Goliath back to the herd!' he exclaimed. After everything he had seen in the last two days, anything seemed possible.

But Jake couldn't have been further from the mark. There was no joyous greeting or friendly gestures as the two elephants reached Goliath. Instead, the bigger of the two, the bull whose trunk Jake had held up for so long, trumpeted menacingly. He stamped the ground with his huge front feet then, holding his head high and flapping his ears, he ran at Goliath, thrusting his lethal tusks at him.

'He's attacking Goliath!' cried Shani, her eyes wide with fear.

With a loud thud, the attacking bull collided with Goliath's flank, sending him reeling backwards. Goliath responded with an anger that secretly delighted Jake. After everything Goliath had been through, it wasn't fair that he should be bullied by a newcomer.

The Musabi bull kicked at the ground, stirring up a cloud of dust then, screaming in rage, he ran at his assailant, meeting him head on. Four tusks clashed with a brittle clatter as ivory met ivory. Locked together, the two young bulls wrestled and twisted, shoving each other back and forth in a menacing dance. The second elephant, meanwhile, stood nearby, watching the attack carefully as if waiting for a chance to join in.

From their tree-top vantage point, Jake and Shani had an unobstructed view. Jake thought that it was almost like watching a wrestling match. Only this fight didn't look much like entertainment. It was obviously much more serious than that. But what was it all about? Goliath hadn't done anything to provoke the attack.

At one point, the attacking bull managed to free his tusks. With surprising agility he slipped out of the way just as Goliath rammed his head at him again. Now the Lufubu bull had the upper hand. With his huge angular forehead, he slammed against the side of Goliath's head, missing his eye by the narrowest of margins.

This was too much for Shani. 'He's going to kill

Goliath,' she shouted, and before Jake could stop her, she scrambled down the tree. 'I'm going to get help.'

'What can anyone do?' Jake yelled after her, but Shani ignored him and went dashing up the path to the house.

The titanic battle continued. Sometimes, Goliath would be at a disadvantage and be driven down the steep slope amid a cloud of dust. At other times, his opponent would be at the receiving end of Goliath's strength and anger, and would have to scramble out of the way.

Meanwhile, down at the river, the rest of the herd seemed not even to notice the fight going on above them. Having drunk their fill, they were now feeding peacefully at the fig tree.

Breathing heavily, the fighters drew apart. They eyed each other coldly then clashed again, their foreheads meeting with an impact that would have sent most animals reeling.

Then, quite unexpectedly, it was all over. Jake saw no outward sign of defeat, no obvious injury or crashing to the ground. Just a slow backing away by one elephant while the other stood his ground, his head held high in an attitude that Jake could only describe as triumphant.

And this, the conqueror, was Goliath!

Jake felt a surge of relief, pride even, at the way the friendless bull had asserted his superior strength. *I wonder what all that was about, anyway?* he asked himself, more confused than ever.

He was still mulling this over, when Shani returned with Rick and Hannah. 'What happened?' Shani called up to Jake.

He climbed down the tree. 'Goliath won,' he said. 'But I still don't know why they were fighting.'

Rick and Hannah studied the three elephants who were now standing together in a clump, their trunks swaying slowly over the dusty ground.

'You'd think they were the best of friends now,' Jake remarked.

'I reckon they are,' Rick agreed unexpectedly.

'You wouldn't say that if you'd seen the way those two were going at each other,' Jake argued.

'Maybe not at the time,' said Rick. 'But right now, these three bulls are as united as they'll ever be. Which was the whole point of the fight.'

'It was?' Shani looked at Rick in surprise.

'Uh-huh. It sounds like Goliath and the other bull were just sparring, jostling for position,' Rick explained. 'And because Goliath came out on top, the other two will respect him now. Elephants are happiest when they know where they fit in the hierarchy.' He beckoned to them. 'Let's get a bit closer,' he said.

They followed Rick to the crest of the hill which gave them a clear view of the three young bulls who were now winding their way down to the river, Goliath walking confidently in front.

Jake was amazed at the way things had worked out. Goliath, the famous loner, had teamed up with two complete strangers! And then Jake remembered what Don had said at Rungwa a few days ago. *Young bulls often roam about on their own until they join up with a bachelor herd.*

'So that's what it's all about. Goliath's formed his own bachelor herd,' Jake said. 'It took him long enough.'

'Maybe he didn't like the other young bulls here,' Shani suggested with a grin. 'Like at school when you're trying to make new friends. There are some people you just can't stand.'

Rick laughed softly. 'Could be, but it's more likely that he was simply waiting for the right time.'

'And perhaps for the confidence of knowing that he belongs to a family after all,' suggested Hannah.

'Bringing Rosa's herd to Musabi was the best thing we could have done.' Jake grinned at Rick as he thought of how many would benefit from the translocation – the other animals in Lufubu once the vegetation started to recover; the villagers living near both Lufubu and Musabi; visitors to the game reserve; Rosa's herd and, most of all, Goliath. But then a grim thought flooded his mind. 'I hope those four poachers don't end up benefiting too.'

Rick looked at Jake and nodded sombrely. 'I'm with you there, Jake. I've just spoken to the police. They're still looking for them, but the trail's gone cold. No one has seen the men since they ran off.'

'I hope they're not hiding somewhere inside Musabi,' Jake muttered, gazing round at the familiar golden landscape.

'I suppose that's always possible,' Rick agreed. 'But I've organized extra guard patrols, and so far they've found nothing unusual.'

'And the other good news is that they haven't found any elephant corpses either,' Hannah smiled at Jake. 'Which means those tusks you found last week couldn't have come from our elephants.'

The news helped to lift Jake's spirits once more. 'With any luck, Goliath gave those four such a fright, they're still running,' he chuckled. He climbed on to a disused termite mound and looked down at the trio of bulls at the bottom of the slope.

Spurred on by the sight of the sparkling water,

Goliath broke into a run and plunged into the river. His new friends charged in after him, and Goliath plunged even deeper into the river until most of his body was submerged. Back and forth he swam, his trunk held high like a periscope.

'I've never seen him so happy,' Jake commented.

'Not even when he's been eating bananas,' chuckled Shani.

Jake nodded. 'And I bet he won't be hanging round us begging for any more!'

Goliath clambered out of the water then looked up to where Jake and the others were standing. Almost as if he was saluting them, he raised his trunk towards them. A deep rumble travelled up the hill, and Jake both heard and felt it through the ground.

'I think he's saying *thank you*,' said Shani softly.

· The vibrating rumble subsided as Goliath turned and trotted over to a nearby mud wallow. He sank down on to his belly, flopped over and rolled luxuriously. Moments later his two friends went squelching in beside him. Soon all three bulls were coated in mud, their grey hides now a rich dark brown so that when they lay still, they were almost indistinguishable from the earth around them.

For the first time since Jake had known him, Goliath looked as if he really belonged in Musabi.

Hannah had photographed the sequence of events. Now she screwed the lens cap back on to her camera. 'Let's go and have some breakfast,' she said, and she and Rick started back for the house.

Jake and Shani lingered at the top of the hill for a moment.

'Come on, you two,' Rick called to them. 'You know you shouldn't stay out here on your own.'

'Coming,' said Shani. She cupped her hands around her mouth. '*Kwaherini, tembos.* So long, elephants,' she called.

Jake stood on the ant-heap and waved. '*Tutaouana,* Goliath,' he called out. 'See you around sometime.' Then he jumped down to the ground and, with the savannah stretched around them in the hot morning sun, he and Shani raced each other back up the path to the homestead.

This series is dedicated to Virginia McKenna and Bill Travers, founders of the Born Free Foundation, and to George and Joy Adamson, who inspired them and so many others to love and respect wild animals. If you would like to find out more about the work of the Born Free Foundation, please visit their website, www.bornfree.org.uk, or call 01403 240170.

PRIDE
Safari Summer 1

Lucy Daniels

Living on a game reserve brings Jake Berman
face to face with animals in the wild. It's exciting
– and dangerous – but Jake's always ready for
adventure . . .

A film company is shooting a movie on the
Bermans' game reserve. It's a chance for
Jake to see what goes on behind the scenes!
But the lion cubs the producer wants to use
have been taken without permission. Jake
soon needs to use all his experience of the
African bush to deal with an angry, injured
lioness . . .

HUNTED
Safari Summer 2

Lucy Daniels

Living on a game reserve brings Jake Berman face to face with animals in the wild. It's exciting – and dangerous – but Jake's always ready for adventure . . .

Jake is thrilled to be going to a chimp conservation area. But gunshots on his first night in the jungle make him realize that it's more dangerous than he thought – and for the chimps most of all. He and his friend Ross are determined to stop the hunters, no matter what the risk . . .